100 Million Oblivion

notionpress.com

100 MILLION OBLIVION

Varun Chopra

notionpress.com

Notion Press

5 Muthu Kalathy Street, Triplicane,

Chennai - 600 005

First Published by Notion Press 2015

ISBN: 978-93-52060-31-3

Dedicated to my father

the late Mr. Sunil Chopra

This book would not have been possible
without his influence.

Sometimes you just have to accept the truth
and move on, to make those people proud,
who love you unconditionally.

His teachings will be my blessings forever.

Author's Note

The inspiration behind the story

I was sitting in my room the whole day reading a book on financial markets and money banking, as my interest in economics had really surged in the last two days. My interest is like a stray dog that roams the streets restlessly and is delighted when it finds a spot of sunlight on a cold day. I had never read a book with so much enthusiasm, at least not when the semester has just begun.

My tendency to get restless returned by night and I sauntered into my friend's room to see if he was interested in playing FIFA. He wasn't in the mood for it so we just lazed around meandering into the usual topics that engineers discuss when they have no goal in sight.

This usually involves turning on Facebook to check out some hot chicks or talking about how we landed up in BITS because we could not crack IIT. Everyone has a story on why they could not crack IIT.

Or, we shift to an existential discussion, like whether God exists or not; What happens after we die; Does reincarnation exist; Why India can't win the next world cup, Can Kejriwal change this country, Modi ji - Ache din aa gaye hai ya jaa rahe hai?

The discussion heats up with everyone taking sides based on their own experiences and usually ends in abuse: "Ch####a kuch bhi bolta hai apne aap se."

(Why do you make up random shit?!)

We hardly ever discussed our topic of study - mechanical engineering. We chose it because we had no other choice.

That day, we did have an interesting discussion. We ended up talking about how life would be if we had 100 million dollars. For the next five minutes, we were totally blank imagining how our lives would change if we woke up next morning and found that we had 100 million dollars.

Just put this book aside for a few minutes and think – what you would do if you had that much money with you.

Would you attend your school or college classes ever again? Would you be following your daily job routine?

We were also confused and did what everyone does, when they're confused.

Googled it.

We had just typed the first two letter of our search "how to..." when the best search engine in the world swung into action. The first result was, "How to kiss?" Why would people research kissing? Is it rocket science? You just need to get close to a girl and the first thing you touch is her lips.

Actually, the first thing can be something else if your girlfriend has 'big' heart.

Eventually, we checked the links on "how to spend 100 million dollars". We stopped for a moment and thought, "Why do we always think in dollars, man? This is not fair. Aren't we being unfair to the other currencies? Why can't we calculate the exchange rate and think in our own currency?" Yet 'dollar' is different. 'Dollar' has certain glamour.

It sounds very cool, '100 million dollars'.

Woah!

Just say it, you will feel good.

We tried researching the pages, but the links were too boring. While we were still messing about, figuring out how we would spend that money, we thought – let's ask our best friends what they would do, with a 100 million.

Strangely, everyone in this world wants money but no one knows what to do, when they actually have it.

You can read thousands of books on where to invest, when to inveOst, how to save, but no one can tell you where to spend the money in order to get that most elusive thing in life - happiness.

Research says that happiness is not determined by how much a person earns but rather, on how they spend it. Some say you cannot buy happiness with money.

People do stupid things when they come into a large sum of money. Even if they've worked hard for it, money often changes people. You'd think it would change people for the better, but unfortunately that isn't usually the case. The more money people have, the more selfish they seem to become.

Money is only good if it's spent. The trick is to spend it on the right things. Spending money on what matters in life will make you happier – seriously.

It's a whole lot better than being completely selfish.

Now the big question arises.

How would you live if you had all the money in the world?

What would you do?

Live in a different part of the world every year; Go up to moon; Buy an island; Cure people; Feed the needy; Donate to charity; Stop a war; Raise the global standard of living; Figure out a way to live forever…

These were the answers we got.

But surely, they were not from the heart!

Imagined responses to an imaginary situation. Just the kind of thing people say who want money, but haven't really asked themselves, even once in their lives, what they would do, if they actually got it.

What people replied when asked what they would do if they woke up to a 100 million dollars:

This was the best part of writing the novel. I literally asked this question to as many people as I could: friends, teachers, just about anyone. Some responses were weird, and some so funny they kept me laughing. This is my shortlist of the best (those which can be published without violating libel and decency laws):

Rohan Rajput (working in Germany) – "I will open a company in Germany where Germans have to learn Hindi, to work in that company."

For all those Indians who are working in Germany and who get rejected just because of the language barrier.

Nisarg Thakkar – "I will check my account again and again. 100 million will look so beautiful."

Yash Chandalia – I will be donating money everywhere around.

Me – "Why don't you donate the money you have right now?"

No reply. Trolled.

Simona – "I will go on a cruise. Yayyy!"

Me – "Why don't you buy the whole ship, stupid?"

Vishesh – "I will die of heart attack."

Jaypee – "Sunny Leone bro, Sunny Leone!"

Chris Takara – "I would set aside 25 mil, so I won't use it, 500K for a party, 20 mil for entrepreneur investment, buy a Ferrari, climb Everest, fuck around for a year and then do serious things!"

Garima – "I will build a house where room designs will change according to the dress I wear."

Hemanshu Sethi – "Lamborghiiiiini!"

Ankur Baheti – "I will make a pool of coins and notes like in the cartoon, DUCK TALES and will swim in it."

Prateek – "I will invade a small country, like a king."

The rest of the responses were not fit for publishing.

Acknowledgement

No task is complete without thanking those who helped you achieve your goals. I would like to give full credit to:

My father - the inspiration behind my life and my creative skills. Though he is not around anymore, his teachings will remain with me forever.

My mother and sister, who always supported and encouraged me through the hard times.

Vipin, Sachin, Pushpa, Ankur Chopra and Rajat Singh and family. All of them enliven our family events and encourage love and bonding within the family.

My maternal cousins and family:

Ankita, Kanika, Evert, Sanchit, Mehak, Vasu, Shivansh, Aastha. All the massis and uncles. Love you guys.

Special thanks to cousins from my father's side; from them we learnt how to achieve our aim in life. IIT, IIM, IAS - they have cleared the toughest competitive exams but remained down to earth. The real mantra behind successful people is humility. They have been inspiring me since childhood. This book would not have been possible without - Vikram uncle, Mona bua, Mahima didi, Vaibhav bhaiya.

Friends are always there to lighten your mood and keeping me in good cheer throughout this book were: Akash

Himanshu, Jatin, Aman, Paras, Shreyak, Sagar my tuition and school friends, and Yash, Ankur, Prateek, Aditya, Anmol, Jyot, Soni, Prakhar, Akshita, Bhagat, Chetak, Rathi, Shashank, Abeer, Anadi, Shreyash and all other my college buddies. Sorry I couldn't name them all.

Now here's a fact that's unbelievable but true: I wrote this novel in three nights. It was no creative frenzy that drove me to push on so rapidly, but imaginative readers who were contributing to the plot.

Chief among these was Master Plotter, Hemanshu Sethi.

I discussed the story with him for hours and we plotted the suspense together. We spent some amazing time, imagining the possibilities of turning this novel into a movie.

The book's cover designers - Neha, Aditya, Rahul and Shreesh.

The main attraction of a book is the cover and they did their best to make it an epic one. Neha displayed her artistry in the sketch, Aditya applied his prodigious imagination, (he designed a metro station and won the first prize nationally) and the minimalistic of all Rahul and Shreesh. They all did a great job.

Soumyaraj Bose - his advice was always on target, whenever the plot got entangled.

Garima Arora who always replied within ten minutes of receiving a new chapter and her replies always made me write the next one. Thank you for the motivation Garima. Our trip to Vegas is due.

Vibhuti Vashishta Sharma, the positive force in my life. I just love telling her stories and her smile always works wonders. I can never tire of life when she is with me.

Tanishka - The best advisor.

Sex scene credits- Sorry guys I have to mention this because you were really awesome. Ankur Baheti and Yash Chandalia - the future of mechanical engineering is in good hands.

Kanishka, Navodita, Faiza, Tannishtha, Sanjogeetha, Namita, Taniya, Jessica and many more girls. Behind every successful man there cannot be a single girl. They all read the story and helped me change the weak parts.

All my professors and teachers – including my English teacher who is probably going to scream after reading this book (Just kidding). I got C grade in TRW and was rated zero in grammar. The point is anyone can write a novel, you don't necessarily have to be good in English. Thanks to the Notion Press team.

I am a storyteller and not a writer, actually.

So I had to cover up in some way.

The last but the most important person is you, the reader.

I have tried my best to make this novel a small but a special part of your life. I hope the characters resonate with you and the book leaves you with good vibes.

Contents

Chapter 1

100 Million Dollar Surprise

Life is a contradiction. Just before you sleep, you look at your alarm with the happy expectation that it will wake you early morning, you will smile, stretch luxuriously, enjoy the cool morning breeze on your face, while you jog or sit on a bench alone, listening to the melodious twitter of birds.

You believe that your whole day will be blessed, your work will be beautifully reorganized with enough time for each job. Everything will go smoothly and your day will be perfect.

But, as we've said, life is a contradiction.

You're woken up in the morning, not by the worst invention in the history of mankind, called 'alarm', but by that annoying, black crow in your balcony that does not find any other fucking place in the world to clear its throat. You shout from your room to shoo away the crow, abuse it in the foulest language, and even try mimicking its raucous voice, but it's of no use. As for that alarm which you so hopefully set last night, you now shut it off with a snarl and a blow!

Research says that it takes us fifteen seconds of intense effort to move from sleep to wakefulness. Well I wish it would work that way with me. I can go back to sleep anytime. Even after I have made the effort to brush my teeth and wash my face, all it takes is for me to enter the bedroom and catch sight of my pillow, as alluring as Sunny Leone begging for a hug, and my bed, as soft and enticing as Britney's belly, and I can't resist diving in.

Welcome to my life! A place where it's becoming harder to concentrate on anything or keep myself motivated. I just end up procrastinating on everything.

Five days back I wanted to be a singer and started taking guitar lessons. God knows why, but the guitar turned out to be a pain in the ass, as well in the hands, so I quit.

At various points I have fantasized that I would be an actor, gamer, hitchhiker, casino owner, website designer, traveler, DJ, VJ and what not.

My interests change faster than time these days, and my mind is preoccupied with a thousand things. I'm not able to focus on what I want from life. I wish I had all the money in the world to pursue my fantasies, but somewhere deep down, I know that even if I did get the money, I will be sleeping, not with a Sunny Leone like pillow but with Sunny herself!

Back to the present. The day begins as mine usually does, with a massive hangover. Along with the usual dizziness and blurred vision I also have a throbbing pain at the back of my head. I look bleary eyed at the date. It is

September 26. Whaaat? The last date I recall is September 10. Days seem to be disappearing on me.

I've been living in this apartment for six months - always planning to shift but never actually doing it, as it will involve the hassle of packing everything up. I am a software enthusiast and an entrepreneur, which is the riskiest combination. There are two types of people with this combination. They are either the richest people in the world, like Steve jobs and Mark Zuckerberg, or people like me, completely broke and lost in life.

As I said I am an enthusiast and not a developer. I cannot even call myself a coder. I just aspire to be one.

I don't remember the last time I hung out with a friend, unless you count that outing to a small bar near our flat, which is our 'Vegas', where the rickshaw pullers play teen patti all night with their hard earned money. As soon as people get high, the bar becomes a casino for them. They bet all the money they earn in a day. For some it doubles, for others, it's all their hard work down the drain.

My life revolves around liquor, coding, half-relationships and gambling.

I know things must change but I just can't seem to motivate myself. And the days just pass while I sit cursing my life, instead of improving it.

I yearn to create something that will change the world. I have no idea what, but I know that it will involve the Internet – the one thing through which I can reach almost anyone in the world.

Friends call me Uday, but my full name is Uday Veer Singh. Girls call me UV. The name seems fit for a king, emperor, fighter or the richest man. But I am none of them. Completely the opposite, you can say.

It's not just the current situation. I didn't have a great time in college either. In fact college life sucked. I graduated with a CGPA so low that no company cared to call me for an interview. It made me want to shout out that marks weren't the only thing that mattered and that I too was capable of contributing to the world. All the crammers and bookworms got placed in different software companies. Posting their status of being '#placed' was the new trend, and the number of 'likes' that followed, was directly proportional to the brand equity of the company hiring them.

Many start-ups were also recruiting and offering high-salaried jobs. Well, seeing your friends getting placed while you're getting nowhere, is the worst thing, actually. You feel low and depressed. I tried congratulating each one whole heartedly, but deep inside, I coveted their happiness. I felt this way even though I had no one in the world to celebrate with me. No parents to applaud my achievements. No brothers or sisters to comfort me in my disappointment.

I told myself that I had a bigger mission than getting placed and working for a company, struggling for increments, sucking up to the boss, and losing myself in the drudgery of chasing a pay cheque.

I wanted to do something big, create something that would live on forever. That's why I pursued entrepreneurship.

But life is not a cakewalk.

I ended up being so fucked up that I'm rarely in my senses these days. Weed, hash, cocaine, LSD, you name it, I've done it. They fill me with possibilities. For a brief while, I feel like a giant with life-changing potential within my grasp. Weed even helps me code better. When I'm on weed I feel like I can code on and on, without a break, like forever.

Last night was another weed trip. Judging by the soreness behind my head I suppose something must have struck me. I have no recollection of what it could be. This is a new low for me. Broke, rejected and dejected. No one to care if I live or died.

To be happy and enjoy life you need money - a lot of it. Though I have never experienced what it can be like to be loaded, I'm convinced that my life will be infinitely better if I have money in plenty.

On my phone are several missed calls from my girlfriend Manika. She thinks I'm a useless jerk because I don't spend time with her. I just call her sometimes when I'm high and heckle her to do something in life. Well, I am her motivation and that's why she talks to me.

Here's an idea. Maybe I can be a philosopher or a motivational speaker, though my own life is a shining example on how to fuck up. Still, I like giving suggestions to people.

I have confided in Manika about my 'mission to improve the world.' I don't know why I'm fooling her. At least I haven't made her any promises about our future, or hinted at commitment. She doesn't expect it of me. That's what I find most attractive about her – the fact that she expects nothing from me.

I don't call her back.

Since I didn't seem to be good at anything else, I thought I would give management a shot. Strangely, everyone thought I could be a great manager. How difficult can it be to designate work to your team, sit in your cabin, signing files and talking on the phone?

Management is what we've been doing since childhood.

I contemplated taking the GMAT but not only was the cost of the exam out of my budget, the fees for international students would swallow the accumulated savings of seven generations of my family!

So CAT is the best option. I'm preparing for it, half-heartedly. Mostly by accessing the Economic Times on my phone, like I'm the Wolf of Wall Street - only this wolf dozes off in seconds!

What I need is a plan for the day. Start with a walk - since I can't afford the gym. Then, clean my room, which is currently more cluttered than a Pharaoh's tomb. Give up drugs, which, let's admit it, I'm addicted to. Finally, apply for a company job and earn a salary to live on. Seriously, I've reached a point where there's barely enough to keep myself alive for couple of months, after which I'll have to start selling my personal stuff.

I had lost a large amount of money gambling, two weeks back, on my birthday. I remembered winning a large sum when I started out, but managed to lose it all by end of day's play.

The writing is on the wall. I need a job or I'll be on the street.

I check the fridge and that's a big mistake. It smells terrible. I try cleaning it out but that only spreads the smell to the whole apartment.

I get a bucket of water to clean the floor, but there's barely a drop of phenol left.

I have no money for cleaning agents. It's a choice between paying the rent and living like a pig, or buying groceries but not having a home to clean.

It's basic psychology. The closer you are to exams, the greater the urge to clean your room, organize your workbench (in my case, the bed), wash your clothes, make Maggi and clear the long backlog of daily chores.

Just excuses to avoid the books.

There is a knock on the door. I quickly throw some clothes over utensils that have no business to be on the bed, and open the door. It's the landlord. He comes three days before the rent is due, just to make sure I can make payment for the month. He always takes my wrist watch, a gift from Manika, and returns it when I pay up. I open the drawer, take the watch out and hand it over. I also gave him a bottle of beer. It's two weeks old and I'm in no mood for it.

He looks at me strangely, unused to generosity.

I have been in debt all my life, scrounging money from every person I know. I hate doing it. The habit of sneaking extra toffees from the shops without paying for them had progressed into reckless borrowing, and then into reckless gambling. This is not who I want to be. Deep inside, I want to be the one to help people around me. To be a giver, not a taker. But I never have enough, even for myself.

I find poverty disturbing. It upsets my emotional equilibrium. Many times, while crossing a road, whenever I see young children, homeless and ragged, begging, I cry. Literally, tears stream down my face. I want to help. I want to change the thinking of people around me. Everyone is so lost in their own world that the world they are living in is lost.

Humanity is heading for extinction if people don't change their priorities. The hunger for power and money, fame and name, has killed off basic compassion and generosity.

Who am I to criticize them? I'm no better. I plan things but don't execute the plans.

I go to the kitchen to check if there's anything to eat. All I can find are some stale biscuits. I eat them.

Where will I find money for food? Where will I find rent money, to keep this roof over my head? I need a plan. My mind runs round and round, in circles, like a rat in a trap looking for an out.

Thoroughly frustrated, I check my bank account using the fastest Internet Wi-Fi in the world, whose modem range is just a little more than an NFC chip.

Do you know what is worse than no Internet?

Slow Internet.

All websites become IRCTC when your net is working slowly. It's so annoying, you'll want to tear your hair out.

I access the interface where I can check my pathetic bank balance. I expect it to show the barest minimum amount. What I see next completely blows my mind. My foot tangles with the bucket of water, which I had brought to clean the room, and I trip. With my foot still stuck in the bucket, I scramble up again to check the screen. This time I trip over the modem cable, which brings my laptop crashing to the floor. The screen is cracked but the figure displayed, is intact.

I roll my eyes, slap myself, but I cannot not believe the entry:

$ 100 million

Chapter 2

Confusion!

The world goes silent. I can hear the drip-drip of tap water echoing in the kitchen sink. My mind struggles to interpret what my eyes saw a few moments back. My heart alternates between pounding with excitement and stopping with shock.

I go into oblivion.

I just could not count the number of zeroes in the figure in front of me. I check again to see if there was indeed a '1' in front of the valueless zeroes. I check, recheck and re-recheck the zeroes. Every time, after counting those zeroes, I go back to the big '1' in front. I have never loved the numeral 'one' as I loved it then.

I take a deep breath, extract my foot from the bucket, and sit dazed and staring on my bed. Okay! This is a prank, or… maybe I'm hallucinating.

To check, I rotate my head fast from side to side. I put the bucket over my head and thump on it to blast the delusionary fogs from my mind.

Was I dead and was this a glimpse of heaven?

Sitting with the bucket over my head, I feel laughter bubbling up. Me? With a 100 million dollars in my bank account? How likely was that? I know drugs can do crazy things to people but this? This is beyond bizarre. Was I in the grip of a massive hallucinogen? Was my mind playing games with me? But, except for the dull throb at the back of my head, I felt completely normal!

I try 2-3 pushups to get the blood flowing and to jumpstart my grey cells. That gave me an idea. Why not check to see if my phone also displays the same amount? I take out my smart phone, another gift from Manika, and try opening the link but it doesn't connect to the Internet.

I realize that the modem cable is disconnected and sodden with water. The modem is just gasps away from extinction. Another possibility strikes me.

I check to see if it is April 1. Do banks celebrate April Fool's Day? Would they pull a prank like this? I didn't think so! Then how did that money come into my account?

Had I done something illegal when I was high??

Was it a mistake by the bank?

My head reels with the possibilities. Many theories enter my mind but with no logical explanation.

I lie tossing on the bed. What would happen next? Was the money real or fake?

How could I suddenly get a 100 million dollars in my account?

I had never seen more that Rs.10, 000 ever, in my life. This was a massive bonanza, as if I had saved President Obama's life and got a reward. It was a 100 million dollars!

How come it's in dollars, man? This is an international bank but how and why will they give me a 100 million in dollars?

Is it like a lottery that my account number has won? Are there any lotteries like that? Crazy shit was going through my mind.

My hands tremble as I open my calculator to multiply 100 with a million and then approximate the currency exchange to be Rs. 60 to a dollar.

My calculator shows 'error' as the figure is more than 8 digits. Even the calculator is showing 'error,' then there must be something wrong, I thought.

What next? I'm gripped with confusion. Should I go to the bank and check? Should I inform them of their mistake? Would they take the money back? Should I go to a police station, instead?

I have no close family or friends to share this momentous news with. I clean my face in the washroom and start pacing around the room. My mind starts projecting images of money around me. I imagine a 100 million dollars in a single room. What will the room look like?

I had barely seen a dollar in my life and now here I was, with a hundred million of them!

An image from my favorite childhood cartoon 'Duck Tales' pops into my mind, where Uncle Scrooge used to take a swim in the money he had. I imagine the same thing in my room. I would love to dive into a 100 million.

I try to clear my head from fantasy. I go back to the questions.

Was this my money? I hadn't checked my account for approximately a month, and now what I was seeing was definitely an anomaly.

I was the poorest person I knew, with no money to live on for more than a month. My room is a perfect picture of what hell can look like. All my dreams, aims, courage were draining away slowly, taking with them the life I wanted to lead.

I had never learnt how to save money and invest for the future. I did not have the proper attitude to respect money. Our attitudes about money are formed in childhood. And it's these attitudes that shape how we use money today.

I had been reasonably well-off before my mom and dad died. My dad worked in the States in a software company - we returned after I was born in the U.S.

I was very young when the accident happened to my parents, and my uncle took all the money away. Since then I have been in India. It took me a long time to recover from that incident and try to live life, but I never learnt how to earn money and how to spend it wisely. I lived for the moment. You only live once (YOLO) was the motto that defined me. None of which explained the huge sum in my bank account.

In the midst of all this anxiety, I hear footsteps on the stairs. I see a shadow pass over the window. Then there is banging on the door and a voice asking me to "Open up!" I imagine being surrounded by police snipers within seconds of opening the door, handcuffed and hauled off to the nearest police station. My heart hammering my chest, I look fearfully through the peephole.

It is the milkman to whom I owe Rs.100 from last week. He vents all his frustration on the door. I just take Rs. 100 from my wallet and give it to him. I add another Rs. 50 and apologize for the delay in payment. He just looks at me in amazement, from top to bottom, as I'm dressed in boxers with Mickey Mouse cartoons on them. It's embarrassing! He's shocked, as I always pay less than what is due, claiming that the milk is diluted with water. We usually spend about ten minutes arguing the point. Today he spends five of those ten minutes just staring, then leaves with a shocked smile.

I pull on jeans and a shirt and resolve to go to the bank and tell them the truth about the money in my account. As I walk my mind is flooded with memories and dreams.

All my life I've always wanted to spend money without a second thought. I just never wanted to worry about it. People spend their life earning it and worrying about it. There are hundreds of people telling you where to invest, when to invest, which property to buy, which bonds to buy, and what not.

Financial advisors earn millions just by giving advice to people. Nobody tells you to live in the moment and spend to be happy.

What if all people can learn to stop worrying about money and live happily?

What if everyone starts to enjoy what he or she has, spend money on themselves and on their happiness?

No power struggles. No comparisons whatsoever. The rich not getting richer. No envy over others' incomes.

Just people enjoying what they have in life. Exploring other cultures and the beauty of nature. I was lost, reimagining the world.

How will I spend that 100 million if I have it for real?

I hold the thought for a second. I imagine myself going crazy with that kind of money, with no tensions.

I cannot not sustain myself for more than a year, with my life in its current downward spiral. But now, suddenly, I had more that I could ever spend even if I lived to be a hundred.

I can buy any fucking thing in this world, I tell myself. My world has been so small but now everything is within my reach:

Going abroad, fucking around for a year, trying the wildest drugs, travelling in the most expensive cars, buying a yacht and a personal jet, girls in bikinis around me all the time, betting in casinos…

After a long time I'm happy, just thinking these thoughts, dreaming these dreams. Just like that I change my mind. Now all I want to do is spend that money.

I don't want to inform the bank. I just want to live my life. I cannot stop dreaming about the life I can live. I'm smiling again. I feel alive again.

I run directly into a cyber cafe to check if I can do any transactions with the money. I research Google on what a million dollars would get me.

I open some of the links:

1. Buy a Lamborghini Aventador and you are broke again.

   I had never bought an Ambassador and now I was thinking about a Lamborghini!

2. DKNY perfume.

   Well, I really needed it to spray in my room. I was planning on buying the cheapest room freshener this morning, and now I was considering a million dollar perfume as room freshener. What a joy!

3. 150 pounds of marijuana.

   Goddamn shit! I'm getting high just thinking about it.

4. Buy Catalina Migliorini's virginity.

   I certainly look forward to this stuff later.

5. 'Gout de Diamants' champagne.

   I can't even pronounce it.

I've never drunk a beer more expensive than a Kingfisher draught and now I can almost taste the champagne on my tongue.

I just wanted to run away after Googling all this. I wanted to leave the ugliness of my life behind. I wanted to live my dream.

I spend another blissful hour checking the best destination for drugs, girls and casinos.

I had heard of this destination only in movies and shows.

I immediately log on to makemytrip.com. This is a good way to check whether my account is working and to make get-away plans.

I don't even need a visa - finally, being born in the U.S would come in use. I don't need a European,Canadian or Japanese visa to travel. Wow. The perks of being an American citizen!

I fill in my details and straight away go in for a business class ticket. I'm nervous whether the transaction would go through.

The cafe owner is staring at me. Is 100 million dollars written on my face? I enter my card details and check again if every digit is right. I reach the final screen and press 'enter' to confirm the booking. It took around five seconds to link to other screen and flash!

'Your session has expired.'

What an anticlimax! For a moment I despair.

Had I taken too much time to enter the details?

Heart pounding, I go for it again, my fingers flying over the keys.

It takes much longer, this time, to reload the final screen. More than ten seconds pass. I close my eyes and pray that the money is for real.

The screen finally responds in bold letters:

'Thank you Mr. Uday Veer Singh.

Your flight to Amsterdam has been booked.'

Chapter 3

How Life Changes!

I rushed from the cyber cafe directly to the most expensive mall in Delhi. I had never frequented the big malls or showrooms in the city, except for a few times. I usually just went to McDonald's, at the entrance of the mall, the cheapest place to fill your stomach.

I had no idea which shop to enter and where to go. Everyone was so well dressed: Husbands and wives dressed western style, with children who looked like they had stepped straight out of an ad, with their expensive clothes and elite diction. They probably even quarreled so politely that one wouldn't even guess that they were fighting!

I was observing everyone while trying to boost my confidence, by looking at my reflection and saying, "Hey will you ever guess that this guy has a hundred million dollars?"

It was time for a make-over, I decided. Let's start with clothing the lower half: shoes, socks, pants, underwear. For me, the last item was the most important. I hadn't bought new underwear in ages and the old ones had faded so much they were completely leached of color.

I began entering showrooms at random, marveling at their names:

'Mango'. Someone had named a store after the humble mango. I expected it to be a fruit shop but there were a hell of a lot of black clothes on display.

I bought everything that looked good to me, without checking the price. The salesman was giving me the evil eye, probably wondering if I could afford the stuff. I don't blame him. In my current get up I was looking terribly ratty.

Louis Vuitton, Versace, Armani, Burberry, Hugo Boss, La Prairie... I just entered showrooms at random and picked up whatever caught my eye.

It took only an hour for my transformation. I began to feel like I was one of those twin brothers in Dhoom 3, the hit Bollywood film, where they looked identical but one twin was suave and the other a simpleton.

By the end of my shopping spree I had gone from simpleton to suave. Along with the clothes, I also donned a new personality. My walk was now a purposeful stride. My voice rang with confidence and my words flowed without a stutter. A haircut, a neat shave and I looked the perfect gentleman.

It was time to experience some new food.

I went to the food court and was confronted by a bewildering variety. People were eating like it was a 'free-for-all' banquet. A fat lady was asking her daughter to bring cholle bhature from the counter. She didn't need a table, she could have balanced her plate on her stomach!

I saw McDonalds, and made a U-turn. It reminded me of all the times when I was forced to fill my stomach as cheaply as possible. I never wanted to go there again.

I noticed that sophisticated looking people, conversing fluently in English on snazzy phones were heading towards Subway. I followed them and I ordered a chicken tikka sub with extra cheese. The guy making it, started asking me what to put in the sub as if I was a chef. Perhaps he was impressed with my get-up and wanted to customize it for me. Strange world. People treat you differently when you are rich.

It was an amazing day for me. My life was going from shit to hit.

I fervently wished that I would never have to return to this life again.

I was happy inside-out. My clothes felt so fine against my skin. They should have a tag on them saying: 'Made in Heaven'.

I prayed to my forsaken Gods just before leaving my room and locking the gate. I had never been a believer, before but now I was proof that miracles do happen.

I gave my house keys to a young boy who was sitting with his old mother outside the park. I asked him to shift into my apartment and take care of his mother. I asked him to open his bag to put some money in it. "Sir don't give this to me," he cried, "I want to earn." I gave him a lakh of rupees and told him to join a school and look after himself.

I held his hands and looked into his innocent eyes that needed to see the better side of this world. I asked him to dream. "Dream about anything you want in this world, and trust me, you will get it one day." He was old enough to understand the magnitude of my advice. I had never donated any money to anyone before, because I had never had any to spare. Now, I was feeling light; my heart was filled with true happiness. For the first time, I was proud of myself. I had explored something different.

"I don't know whose money I am spending but I will just do what I think is right," I resolved. I wanted to help people as well as expand my horizons. I wanted to make mistakes and learn from them. This was a chance for me to see life beyond poverty, I wanted to try everything once, and then make a judgement. I wanted to help those around me, whoever I could. I was rich now. I was ready for a completely different life.

I entered the airport and put on the earphones, plugged into my brand new phone. I hadn't put any songs on, so I just listened to the FM. Some random old songs came on so I changed the station immediately.

There was a traffic announcement, followed by local news. One item caught my attention:

"A 23 year old man named Abhi was found dead in his home near Dwarka Sector 11. He killed himself by setting his house on fire. The police and fire brigade reached the destination in time, but the house was almost completely burnt down. His mother, who had been a cancer patient for the last 6 months, had passed away five days earlier. According to hospital sources, the victim had been mentally disturbed after his mother died. The police have declared it a case of suicide."

I tried recalling someone named Abhi. I had heard the name before. I wondered where. I hardly knew anyone in Dwarka Sector, besides my milkman and landlord.

The minutes ticked by and finally... it was time to go to Amsterdam!

A Business Class seat should be called a 'sex chair,' actually. You can just lie down on it and the cushion will make you feel orgasmic. I wished everyone would close their eyes so I could masturbate on it freely.

It had been ages since I had watched porn. Just the thought charged me up and I started chatting up the airhostess.

She was from Bulgaria. I had no idea where the hell that was, but I acted like I did. She asked me whether I had been there before. I was not expecting that.

I lied and told her that I had visited the country when I was a child and had vague memories of it, and that I would love to join her there some day. I have not gone two streets farther than my house by myself and now Bulgaria. Woohoo!

I would have loved to flirt longer but some asshole buzzed for her. She went off to deal with him.

She was wearing a tight skirt through which her panty line was clearly visible. That triggered off all kinds of chemical reactions in my body. I could imagine her perfect shaped ass with its asymptotic curves touching each other.

Life should actually freeze at such moments and you should have a power to zoom into it.

Reality, like this, can be more arousing than soft porn.

Her name was Jessica. I loved her name. It sounds so seductive. She came back and we started talking again. She told me about her life as an airhostess, and how she lived alone in Bulgaria, as she valued her independence.

She supported various NGOs around the world and her aim was to build a school for International students where people could learn entrepreneurship. She was very active in helping society in any way possible. She was helping ten disabled students learn football, a game they loved. In short, she was leading a full life.

I gathered that she had joined the aviation industry because she wanted to explore different cities and live freely. She liked to meet new people and she got to do that every day, on this job.

She loved the piano and hated dogs. She told me a story of how a dog had bitten her on the back of her thighs.

I pictured it in my mind. Just a little higher and the dog would have marred the allure of that majestic ass.

I would then have hunted down that bloody animal in Bulgaria, and left him on the Indian streets with our stray dogs. He would have learnt the lesson of his life.

Yes, I just love our dogs. They will never allow any other dog into their territory. Every one of them will surround and attack the stranger, like the U.S army attacked Osama.

I felt like I had made a friend after a long time, and I could have chatted on and on. I wished Jessica could accompany me, though I also wanted to enjoy the beauty of the city alone. You know I'm referring to the 'internal beauty' that I had searched for on the Internet.

We talked for another hour about all the things I must do while in Amsterdam.

That's when she told me a secret that she had never revealed to anyone before. Amsterdam has a well- known red-light area, which attracts hookers from all over Europe. When she first came to Amsterdam she had no money, so she had worked in the red light district. She told me that she still had many friends there and could arrange a special discount if I was interested.

I knew money was not an issue anymore but if her friend were as sexy as her, then I was definitely looking forward to it.

I quizzed her on how to score drugs in the city. She named a coffee shop that was present in every third street in Amsterdam. In India too it's not that difficult. You just need to see a rickshaw stand and a paanwale, find the smallest street nearby and you will get lucky.

But the main difference was drugs were 'legal' in Amsterdam. The only time the word 'LEGAL' has happy connotations is when it is applied to 'SEX', 'DRUGS', 'RAVES'.

Man, what a dreamland! In India we had to conceal even beer bottles in our cars, while here the scene is crazyyyyyy!

Every third shop is a sex shop or a coffee shop or a casino. Amsterdam – The heavenly hell!

Once when she was high on weed, in her early days in the city, she had started stripping off in a night club.

That story excited the hell out of me. I could feel the devil dancing in my head as I visualized her striptease. I wanted her to come with me now, at any cost.

She said she was busy for a day, but she would be in the Red Light area the day after that. Why man, why does she arouse me like this?

Once the flight landed, all I wanted to do was sleep, It had been a long journey and I had spent the night yakking. I came out of the airport and looked at the beautifully lit up city. This place was so different from India, it was like landing on a different planet.

I took a selfie with the big white board that read AMSTERDAM at the entrance to Schiphol Airport.

I boarded a bus with a weird hotel name on it. I had no idea what language people spoke in the Netherlands. 'Kh' 'Kh' is all I could hear around me. They should start gargling in the morning, I thought.

I was transported to my hotel royally and fell into a quick doze. Just as I was switching off the light, I saw a card advertising massages, on the bedside table. My eyes flew open and in a trice I had 'Reception' on the line. I asked for details. The receptionist mentioned a 'naughty massage' and that was enough to drive away every last bit of sleep.

The stress of the last three days simply vanished. I lay down the on the bed in the horniest pose I knew, to attract the massage girl. Actually, boys should not try it. They look too weird.

Why don't we have such beds at home I wondered? So fluffy, so cozy, you can make love to them. Within a minute there was a knock on the door and a girl holding a plate with oil and other supplies, entered.

I just couldn't take my eyes off her. She was way taller than me with long blonde hair. I had seen such a girl only in porn movies and now here she was, live in front of me. She dressed like a waitress, in uniform, with an apron tied behind her neck. It was my wildest fantasy come true.

The softness of her hands could set the standard for silk. She rubbed them slowly down my back. Then massaged my shoulders and lower back with passion. She then climbed on my back. It was mind blowing! She was awesome!

Her weight on my back was indirectly pushing my penis into the bed and the feeling was super orgasmic!

She bent down and trailed her breasts over my back. I shuddered in ecstasy. She was bombarding me with pleasure.

Somewhere I felt guilty about spending money that I had not earned, in a manner not entirely ethical.

I wished I knew where the money had come from.

I never wanted that massage to end, ever. It was pleasure, pleasure, pleasure all the way.

Naughty, Naughty, NOBODY DOES IT BETTER!

I could feel myself float away. At some point I fell asleep. I will resent that sleep for the rest my life.

Chapter 4

Eat Sleep Crave Repeat

My plan was to spend no more than a day at each destination. This way I could try out different drugs and different chicks in different places.

I suited up for the day in jet-black with a sharp tie and I was ready to roll. I went down to the lobby to choose which car I would hire for the day. The masseuse chick was standing there, making eyes at me, caressing her lips with her fingers, trying to arouse me again. She had taken an extra 100 euros from my wallet when I'd converted the 'naughty massage' into a 'horny massage'. I responded by putting my fingers on her lips and asking her to stay chill out.

In reply, she bent forward a little to show me her cleavage, which I hadn't observed closely last night. Why God? Whyyyyyyyyy? Why do girls look so hot in clothes with a bra on, and not so hot when you actually see them naked?

This is the biggest weapon that women have that can drive a man out of his senses. A man will promise the earth and the moon, when a girl seduces him with her cleavage. I shook my head to clear these nonsensical thoughts away.

They showed me the cars they had with them. Till now my usual mode of transport had been DTC buses, with people hanging from them, or Share Auto's crammed with strangers. Now here I was with a choice before me - Porsche, Lamborghini, Rolls Royce and Jaguar. I choose a flame-red Jaguar.

It had an air of quiet luxury that appealed to my senses. Its fine leather caressed my body. Polished wood veneers gave it a touch of class. It whispered of meticulous attention to detail by the world's finest suppliers. It had amazing legroom.

The masseuse was still making eyes at me so I took her along for an extra 500 euros. If the scenery was a let-down then she could always entertain me with her moves. She sat near me with the top buttons of her shirt undone, to give me a good view of her curves. I pulled her close and buttoned her up. I was in no mood to play.

My first stop was Madame Tussauds, which had wax statues of famous celebrities, made to seem completely real. Everything was a novelty to me. I took pictures of each and every celebrity. Maybe, someday my statue would be amongst theirs. The overnight millionaire!

It was time for some fresh beer. There was this place called Heineken where the beer breweries were established. The beer was literally AWESOME!

The thing I like most about beer is that it will make you happy all the time. Drink beer and it will bring out the best stories in you. You brim with good cheer and a love of mankind.

If water was replaced with beer, the world would be a much happier place. Fresh beer has an intoxicating smell. It keeps your testosterone pumping. I don't know if that last fact is true, but in my case it felt it like someone was tickling my testicles.

The place had an ethnic feel to it with the beer kept in large wooden kegs and everyone being served in large mugs. People over seventy years of age were also enjoying their life, sitting around with young people and remembering their heydays. They were as lively as they had been in their youth.

Time to move on. Now it was time - to explore the city's best attraction.

RED LIGHT DISTRICT AND COFFEE SHOP-

World's best combination

I entered the coffee shop and there was whole list of joints available, more than thirty of them. Wow! I gave the guy at the counter a hundred euros to give me best joint he had. I could smell the pot in the air and my body was desperate for it. He rolled the joint. Three drags and my world was upside down. Man, it was powerful. The best high I have ever had. I was on a roller coaster; I could not stand still. I needed music, lights, strippers.

Every drag sent a power surge through my body. I could feel it coursing through my veins. My hands were going numb. I didn't know what was happening to me. I do know one thing, once you start tripping, whatever you do, you keep doing over and over.

If you laugh, you keep laughing for hours. If you get sentimental, you cannot stop crying.

As for me, I was in the RED LIGHT DISTRICT.

There was only one thing I could keep doing!

The whole place is so arousing – it's like your sex organs are on steroids. Maybe he had given me Ecstasy or some sex drug – but I was going out of control seeing the girls around me.

All your fantasies can come true here.

On the first floor I could see a guy completely chained by a girl, who was on her knees facing him and eating a lollipop. She was hitting him with a whip. It was all madness.

You know, this place is like a sex restaurant where you can order what you want. Each girl is inside a cabin which has a glass door with a red light shining inside, which gives it its ambience. If you stand in front of the door, the girl will open it and entice you in her most seductive voice. She will lower her bra just enough to give you a glimpse of the pink of her nipples, ask you to explore the rest of her by 'cumming' in. Once in, out comes the Menu:

Fantasy, Posing, Wild Night, Strip Sex, Naughty massage…

I was just talking to the girls at random, searching for the best one. I wanted a real beauty who would blow my mind, apart from just blowing.

I saw a tall blonde dressed in a police uniform.

I don't know about you, but once I eyeball an ass I just remember it. It was the same ass with the same panty line and I was a goner!

JESSICA

She had told me she had worked here sometime back. I didn't know she still did. This was turning out to be the best night ever. Dreams do come true. I just took her inside the room without asking for a price. I was turned on by the police uniform.

She ripped my shirt off careless about the buttons, while I unbuttoned her tight shirt slowly, working each button open. I saw her cute belly button which sported a piercing with a ring on it. I slipped my hands onto her smooth belly and I could feel her excitement building up. With every passing second her breath grew heavier. I slowly moved deep into her thighs, which turned her on.

I was flying high!

I then slid my hands into her bra, slowly feeling each and every inch of her skin.

(I could see her breasts peak.)

Her nipples were hard.

I could see the impression of her nipples through her bra.

I slowly lay on her, feeling her smooth, soft skin.

I pressed her hard against my body and with that something grew harder.

She was wearing a special bra called Balconette. She told me it's a kind of 'shelf' designed to lift the breasts to enhance their appearance, shape, and cleavage.

It's like sitting in a balcony from where you can get the best view of the movie.

While she was explaining all this her hands were caressing her breasts. I asked her to, "…shut the fuck up and come to bed." I have no fucking interest in bra details. I'm not a bra distributor.

I'm more interested in knowing the inside story.

She took my pants off and sat on my lap with her sexy breasts near my face. My eyes were wide open.

If life came with a 'pause' button I would have frozen on that moment forever.

It was hormonal!

I could hardly believe what was happening. My hormones were raging out of control. I just wanted to make love to her right then.

I slowly took off her jeans to feel her soft white legs that had the perfect amount of fat on it.

Actually, she had perfect amount of fat everywhere on her body.

If you know what I mean…

She had a tattoo on her back that said, make love.

And it all started.

It was slow in the beginning but she was wild later on. I gave her my best shot, hell yes, I did!

Her screams incited me even more. I was making love to my dream girl. But, this was beyond any dream.

This was my best night.

The naughtiest night.

Yet again, nobody does it better than in Amsterdam.

She said, "You are my tiger," and bite me on my neck.

"You are fast, hard, ferocious and strong!"

I was proud.

It was 3 a.m. and time for a rave.

We found a party. It was like Zombie land. Everyone was stoned and wasted. We took a hit of a drug that Jessica bought from a bald, black guy who slipped her a packet.

It went straight up the nose and hit my brain so hard that I could not see anything for five seconds. I was stunned.

We were holding each other for support, wandering down the road, entering random hotels and talking to random people.

People become so friendly after taking drugs. They talk so politely with you. Or, maybe it's the other way round.

You start enjoying every second of your life.

The last thing I remember before entering a club where I couldn't even hear myself, was that I was not wearing pants.

But I just entered and then, bang!

You know what the best part is? That you don't remember the worst part.

Chapter 5

Bad Dreams

My head was spinning. My eyes seemed to be glued shut. Somewhere I knew something was wrong. Scene after scene was flashing through my mind.

I had no control over my thoughts. They were disturbing.

Flashback

I hear a gunshot. The rest of the image is fading. I can't see anything.

Change of Scene

A deep sonorous voice is saying – "I knew money would change you. You were a bastard and I knew it, but I had no other choice." He is addressing someone standing in front of him but I cannot see who it is. The scene is ominous. Something bad is about to happen.

And then… it disappears.

Change of Scene

"This plan will surely work. We have done the simulation a thousand times. It's not going to fail. You need the money. We both need money. This is the only way out. Sometimes you have to go against your principles to achieve something. C'mon we can pull this off."

Change of Scene

The MGM Grand. I can see myself.

I'm happy, I don't know why.

I look high.

I woke up suddenly in a pool of sweat. Jessica was in bed with me. I shifted her arms to move out of the bed and she came awake, smiling.

Jessica told me that I had been sleeping for thirty six hours. She had put me in a bathtub fearing a drug overdose. A friend had helped shift me from tub to bed when I'd started shivering with the cold.

I had no recollection of the last three days.

Drugs had blown away my mind and brought on the bad dreams. Bad dreams had haunted me for a while, after my parents died. I struggled to recall coming to this hotel.

The last thing I remembered was dancing to the song,

"Don't you worry child." I was standing on the bar and everyone was cheering me on. Jessica told me that it was because I was standing up there naked.

I was mortified. The best thing about drugs is not remembering anything. Even if someone tells you exactly what you did, you will try to picture it and fail. You don't believe things that you don't remember. At least that's what I told myself.

She also told me how we got to this hotel. Apparently I had been pulling money out of my bag in handfuls, shoving it at total strangers, hollering: "Take it! I have enough for seven generations. Take it and enjoy your life!"

Her voice was low and sweet: "You were completely crazy," she said, "You kissed girls at random and told every girl that she was the most beautiful lady you had ever seen."

Now that I wish I had remembered. They all looked so beautiful. They all looked similar, blue eyes, blonde hair, red lips and soft voice.

It's really cool, when the girl you like is talking about you, flirting with other girls, and she has no problem with it, whatsoever. Maybe she didn't feel the same way about me, and that is why it didn't matter to her.

Finally she had brought me to this hotel, 'Le Chatelaine', and put me in the tub with the shower on, to bring me back to my senses.

"I changed your clothes and tucked you in. After that, you slept like the dead. Truly! I even checked your heartbeat from time to time. Finally I fell asleep with my hands on your chest."

At her words a cartoon heart popped out of my heart. Lovebirds twittered around my head. Heart shaped bubbles appeared in my vision, filled with cupids blowing kisses. I could smell love, taste love and feel love all around me.

Why did I wake up? I should have died in her arms

I didn't want to share this cheesy, romantic stuff.

So I replied, "You had a flight… why did you miss it?"

"I couldn't leave you like this, you couldn't even stand."

I took her hand and closed my eyes. No one had ever taken care of me. What she had done was completely unexpected. I knew Jessica would be a good friend but I'd stopped expecting anything from anyone. She got this funny look on her face and told me to "Man up!" and ditch the sad stuff. I feel like hugging her and I did, wrapping her in my arms and holding on for a long time.

After a long time I felt the power and value of bonding between people. I did not love her but she was the only one I had in this world. I wished I could tell her what she meant to me.

It's funny how you can tell when someone likes someone else, but you can't tell when you like someone!

I brushed my teeth after like, three days! Freshened up. My eyes still felt heavy and my lips were super dry. I ordered an orange juice and an omelet. I let myself relax. It was a different feeling, coming back to my senses after such a long time.

I was preoccupied with the dreams that I had had this morning. I tried to figure out whom I was talking to and who else was there with me? I could not recall a single face.

But I had heard a gunshot! Who got killed and what happened after that?

Was it my imagination or had somebody been killed? I had had bad dreams before but not like this.

This time, I was in my dreams.

I tried to tell myself that the dreams were probably drug-fuelled hallucinations. Maybe I should relax for few days, eat healthy and detox. It was time for a different kind of life now.

Time to try different cuisines and food. Time to live a normal life. Maybe I didn't need this much money.

I was just spending it recklessly. It was high time I got my act together.

I wanted to explore the peaceful part of the continent, away from these fake thrills.

Of what use are drugs? They don't teach you any good thing about life. They're just temporary fun. They create a craving that you're ready to die for. What are you left with get when you come back to your senses? Regret!

I didn't want regret in my life now. I had satisfied some of my cravings but deep down I knew that the path I was on, was the road to nowhere. Life taught me life.

It was time to see the real beauty of the world; the real happiness.

Jessica and I had each bought a Euro Pass to roam around Europe. The hedonistic part was over. Now I wanted beauty and calm.

Jessica planned it all:

France, Italy, Spain, Germany, Greece, Sweden, Switzerland.

We took the best seven, chosen by her. It was all new to me so I had no preferences.

I wanted to feel the power of nature and the strength of silence. I wanted to sit at a cliff's edge and feel the wind whipping around me. When the wind roars in your ears it's like hearing the voice of God.

We went everywhere - by cycle or on foot.

We were on a trekking tour of Europe. We researched the best trekking places in every country. Each one had a different feel. Every trek is like a fresh start; you will find different challenges, a different experience for your senses.

I began to love trekking. On the long hikes I got to thinking about life. Actually, treks are like the journey of life.

You will find some stony paths, you will tire, you will enjoy the rest after the hard work, you will dream about the place you want to reach and eventually you will get there.

I would go and sit on the highest cliffs and ponder existential questions:

Why was I born? What is my aim in life?

What happens when we die?

Even while I asked myself these questions, I knew I would not seek too deeply for the answers. Those who think about death never really live.

One day we were trekking in Italy, on the huge Dolomites mountain range; Alta Via 1. We were enjoying the trek as always. Every journey gave us new friends and new people to talk to.

Everyone is so cheerful when they are trekking.

Sometimes a passing smile from a stranger can touch your heart so deeply.

The confidence, strength and change in the attitude of trekkers returning successfully from the peak, motivates you so much.

I just stopped Jessica in the middle of trek to ask her a question that had struck my mind:

I asked her what she would do if she were to die today.

She replied with a smile, that she would watch as many comedies as possible, as she wanted to die happy!

Her answer rocked me. Each and every hair on my body stood. I knew I was face to face with a big truth:

What I was searching for in the world, was within me.

Your happiness is in your power. You can create it from within. Every person has their own definition of happiness. Your mind recognizes it. You just have to bring it out.

We sat on the highest peak holding each other's hands.

I was falling for her.

Day by day our bond was deepening. Second by second. We explored different cultures. We tried different cuisines. We just loved each other's company.

In this, the most peaceful week of my life, I discovered the true meaning of happiness.

I wanted to tell her that I loved her but always drew back at the last moment.

I don't remember how many times I had told her that I loved her when I was high, but now, without drugs and alcohol, I lacked the courage to say the words.

Which brought me to the million dollar, or should I say, hundred million dollar question.

What attracted her: My money? Or me?

I wish I could tell her about the money. The 100 million that changed my life.

Flashback

"We did it man!

I told you it would work. You were awesome.

100 million dollars in fucking fifteen days!

Goooooooooosebumps!"

I was crying! I have never earned money in my life and now...

Change of Scene

"You want to kill me, then shoot me, but I am not lying!"

Gunshot.

Chapter 6

Feelings!

I had this bad dream that woke me up in the middle of the night. I woke up sweating, with a throbbing head. I tried concentrating on the images, but my headache intensified.

The truth is they felt more like recollections than dreams... as if all of it had happened to me. I could recall words, the hint of a face… A tall man heavily bearded, brown eyed. He had this scar on his face and he was bleeding. He was crying and saying something.

He had a gun in his hands.

He was pointing it at me.

Why would anybody try to kill me? I explored the possibilities.

Was it a vengeful relative?

Was money the motive?

Was it déjà vu…an echo from a past life?

Or a premonition… a vision of someone trying to kill me in the future?

My thoughts were galloping in all directions. I tried to recapture some of the day's calm. All I wanted was peace. What was happening to me?

Sometimes all you need is tender loving care and Jessica was dishing it up in spades. I couldn't help but fall in love. She was there at the right time, doing all what I wanted her to do. If only I could rid myself of these bad dreams, life would be perfect.

People with money are haunted by the fear of losing it.

Since my money was not really mine, my fears were even worse!

I saw Jessica as the solution.

I decided to tell her that I loved her. But I want it to be in some place special. A place so magical that people dream of visiting it at least once in their life. A place where the lowly cares of the world vanish. A place to cherish and remember forever.

I want to give her the most unforgettable moment of her life.

I turned to Google. I typed, "Most romantic places" and it auto filled the rest.

The most romantic place in the world, to propose to a girl was - Las Vegas.

I booked two tickets immediately.

I wanted it to be a surprise for her, so I made up a story that I had to rush to Las Vegas to help out a friend. I asked her to join me on the trip. She demurred saying that she had been away from home for too long. But I knew that there was nothing waiting for her back there. That's women for you - they expect men to ask them a hundred times, cajole them, pamper them and what not, before they give in.

Men are equally idiotic. They are ready to ask them a hundred times. If you ask your sister once, and she says 'no' to you, "Bhaad mein ja" (Go to hell!) springs to your lips. But there's a different rule for girlfriends.

I groveled, pleaded and cajoled till she finally agreed to come with me.

What Happens in Vegas

☺

The aircraft broke through the thin layer of white clouds floating above the ground. A streak of sunlight strayed through cabin window and rested on my left cheek. The heat stirred me awake. Disoriented, I thought for a while that I would find myself in that decaying old apartment near the "Desi Daru Theka" back in Delhi – I trembled at the thought of having to wake up and find some work to pay for the evening beer.

I rubbed my eyes and peered through the window at the expanse of blue surrounding the craft. And then I became aware of a gentle weight on my shoulder. Jessica was quietly sleeping, resting her head on me, her breath as innocent as a newborn's, as calm as the summit of a mountain.

Tears welled in my eyes. How could I possibly tell her the truth about the money? What if she doubts my character? What if she leaves me?

I flipped through the pages of the in-flight magazine. My teardrops fell on a page that read in bold letters: "LAS VEGAS: LIVING IN THE SEA OF NEON."

I flipped through the magazine quickly, to get away from my demoralizing thoughts. Page after page bore pictures of casinos, people dressed in expensive party-wear betting their lives on a stack of chips and a few shiny dice, and exotic dancers, dressed to the bare minimum, entertaining appreciative guests, with their shimmies.

I had really grown up in the last couple of weeks. Such pictures, especially the last one mentioned, would have had the old me, rushing to the toilet and locking myself in, until the last drop of sexual pleasure was wrung from my body. But not this time. I stayed put, holding on to the only thing in the universe that I cared for, as she shifted silently on my shoulder.

The plane hit an air-pocket. The seat-belt signs came on. "Is everything alright?" Jessica inquired, with her eyes only half open. "Yes, darling. Everything is." I put the magazine away and gently leaned my head on hers. I brushed my fingers through her hair, I kept mumbling, "Everything is going to be alright."

I had booked the most expensive hotel in Vegas to make it a very special day for her.

She began speculating on where we were heading. I asked her relax and trust me.

We landed in the airport and a limo was waiting to take us to the hotel. She was all smiles and hugged me tightly:

"You think I have no idea what's going on, stupid?" she said affectionately. "Did you think I would really buy that story about your friend needing you out here?"

I didn't know how to react to that. I was glad that she seemed all right with the idea of commitment but a little secrecy would have been more fun.

But, she was smiling; she was excited.

We entered the hotel and were greeted with free drinks.

We were both smiling and enjoying the buzz.

The best suite on the Strip has a fabulous rotating bed with mirrors on the ceiling, its own glass elevator to the second floor, an infinity pool with the Playboy logo on the bottom, massage room, screening room, private gym, eight-person hot tub and a sauna. That was our suite. It also had killer views of the city.

The whole beauty of a modern city is completely different compared to the beauty of a city with ancient sculpture and historic buildings. That's the difference in ambience between the U.S and Europe. Both places have their own charm.

But the main charm was Jessica.

She was all I wanted from life now.

I put on a blue tuxedo and a bow. I wanted to be the perfect prince for the princess.

She emerged dressed. She looked flawless. I stood silently marveling. She had an oval shaped, beautiful face with glowing skin. Her nose was arrow straight. Not even an iota of dimensional error.

She radiated natural beauty. The kind you get without make up. Dark curving lashes framed wide innocent eyes that were a light greenish-blue. Her eyebrows were perfect arches. Lustrous strawberry blonde hair completed the picture. She was model perfect.

Her natural beauty made you want to look at her forever. It was matched by her radiant personality. Whenever she smiled, she smiled happiness!

She came up to me and put her hands in mine. We were ready for a night on the town. We got into our waiting white limo and I asked the driver to take us to the most expensive casino of the city.

The city's lights dazzled and everyone was lost in their own bubble of happiness. We were going to have the best night of our life in this city. The city where people dream of spending a night.

As the saying goes:

What happens in VEGAS stays in VEGAS.

The limo came to a halt. I stepped out and looked around. Right in front of me was this giant signboard. Dazzling lights spelt out the words:

'MGM Grand'

I suddenly felt a piercing pain at the back of my head. I could feel Jessica take my hand in hers.

Flashback

I am standing exactly at the same spot. In front of MGM Grand. But what am I doing here and who are these people with me?

One of them is a girl.

She is my girlfriend from Delhi. Manika.

My head burned like red-hot fire.

***

Suddenly there is a splash of water on my face.

A security guard was helping me to my feet.

Jessica was in tears distressed by the situation. I hugged her tightly and tried to calm her down. I was about to relate my dream, when the guard turned to me and said:

"You haven't returned to your country, sir?"

Chapter 7

The 100 Million Dollar Owner

I could not believe what the guard was saying. Me? Here before? Even Jessica was flummoxed.

I was desperately trying to puzzle out the scene again but my head was spinning. The questions went round and round:

Was this something that had happened to me in a past life? Had I been here in another incarnation?

Another possibility struck me. Did I have a twin brother whom mom and dad had hidden from me? Why would they do that? What would he be doing here?

My situation was getting more improbable by the minute.

I questioned the guard: When had he seen me before? Who had I been with? What exactly had he seen?

He answered politely:

"Sir, I see thousands of people here, every day. I remember your face because you used to give me a 100 dollar tip daily. This was around two weeks back, when you were here with a friend and a girl.

The last time I saw you, you were leaving the casino for your hotel and then your lady came out and followed you. That's all I know sir."

This was surely not possible. This could not be me. Two weeks back I was in Delhi frustrated with my life, how could I have been here? I had never even heard of MGM Grand before.

Then again, the money, the dreams, the headaches… Something was drastically wrong. Jessica was stroking my back and making soothing noises.

"Do you know that everyone in the world has seven people who are exact look-alikes?"

She was trying hard to comfort me, but I didn't know what to think.

We entered the casino. I didn't want the night to be entirely ruined. The place was well lit with shimmering crystal lights perfectly placed along the bottom of the wall, glancing light across it.

It reminded me of a setting from Titanic, with its majestic chandeliers and dazzling blue water cascades.

Slot machines ran the length of the casino, completely occupied by people. Some were losing, some were winning, but everyone was having a grand time.

Actually people don't mind losing money in Vegas. The ambience is so well designed, to keep your mood high and rolling.

This place never sleeps. It was late at night and it was as bright as day. Waiters were serving the finest whisky in the world. Exotic dancers were jiving to the beats of Congo bongos and a band was performing Coldplay songs. Vegas lives up to its reputation as entertainment capital of the world.

We ordered two glasses of finest red wine on the roof of the casino, from where we had a great view. Las Vegas shimmered at our feet. The wine was of a fine vintage, smooth and mellow. I felt my mood begin to elevate. The dark night and the discreet lighting wove romance into the air. And, when our palate is flooded with generous measures of the finest alcohol, it intensifies the pleasure.

I was looking into her beautiful eyes; we were carrying our glasses and standing near the edge of the building. The view was perfect for a proposal. She had a tiny mole on her neck, which I could see, above her diamond necklace. The alcohol was making me romantic. Some occasions call for a little dizziness.

I had a ring with me that I wanted to give her. I took the glass from her hand and brought the ring out of my tuxedo pocket. A pearl of a teardrop glistened in her eyes. Her face grew lustrous with love. The ring, the moon, the city lights paled in comparison.

There was a drop of wine clinging to her upper lip, which I could not resist. It was the best kiss ever. It was passionate, it was loving and it was endless. My heart brimmed and I knew she was the right one for me.

She said yes!

My happiness was tempered with niggling guilt. I had invited her to share my life but I had failed to share its most important secret. The money we were spending was not mine. Of course I had to tell her.

How would she feel about it? Would she still love me?

I couldn't have given her these moments without money. I wouldn't even have met her without it.

Two weeks back money was the most important thing in my life. But now I had my love. Money can give you part-time happiness but for lasting joy you need to be loved.

Still, I had to out find whose money it was.

There were several interconnected casinos in the building. High on emotion, Jessica and I held hands and went from one place to another. We reached a casino where everyone was silently playing the game.

There were tables all around and people were drinking and losing money. We could see a big flashing board.

TEXAS HOLD'EM POKER

Flashback

The guy, who was with me at the entrance of the MGM Grand hotel? He was now sitting at the table before me and a dealer was dealing out cards. Even the name board was the same - Texas Hold'em Poker!

Scene Change

"Friends like you can only be found by luck!"

Gunshot.

Scene Change

I am standing outside a room. I can hear whispering inside. The place is unfamiliar. I open the door. I see a girl holding a guy's hand and bending over him. It was Manika! I run out in anger.

***

I woke up in my hotel room with Jessica standing over me. It was time tell her about the money. My secret was destroying me. I told myself that she would stay, and that she loved me with her whole heart.

I couldn't summon the energy to get out of bed. Jessica saw my eyelids flutter and brought me water. Once again I heard about how I had lost my senses and how she had brought me to the hotel. My first priority was to contact Manika and find out if she knew anything.

Jessica hadn't slept all night so I encouraged her to take a nap and I left the room to make the call. I could remember Manika's phone number easily, as she was the only person I spoke to regularly, in Delhi.

She picked up the phone.

"Hello, who is this?"

"It's me, Uday."

"Where are you Uday? I've been looking for you all over. I went to your place and found a boy and an old lady in your apartment. They told me you'd left. Where are you? Do you know Abhi is no more? He committed suicide! Tell me where you are, right now!"

"Who is Abhi?" I asked.

"Your best friend Abhi! Don't act like you don't know him. He was your best friend. It was a misunderstanding, I told you. But tell me, is the money safe with you? You earned those 100 million dollars."

I was jolted. "I earned those 100 million dollars?" I felt myself blacking out.

Chapter 8

Memory

I woke up in the hospital with the now familiar throb in my head. I tried recalling the conversation I had with Manika.

She said it was I who earned the 100 million dollars.

How did she know I had 100 million? Who else knew about this?

How on earth did I earn a 100 million suddenly, when until then I had earned barely enough to eat?

Who was Abhi?

I could see Jessica and the doctor standing in the next room talking to each other. I was shaken by what I had learned. How could I forget money that I had earned?

My twin theory had been shot down. Manika had confirmed that it was I who had earned it. Would I have spent so recklessly if I knew it was my own hard earned money?

The doctor came in and sat beside me. He looked grave.

Jessica was tearful. I had a bad feeling about this.

The doctor showed me an MRI of my skull and indicated an area that had a lesion. He said that I suffered from a condition called Retrograde Amnesia resulting from a traumatic brain injury such as a sharp blow to the head.

The blow had caused a thalamic lesion which meant that my memory loss was selective. While I was able to provide autobiographical information about my past, I would be unable to recall events relating to a specific incidents around the time of the injury.

There was no medical treatment for Retrograde Amnesia. Fortunately, he said, memory could be recovered and the recovery is usually spontaneous and gradual. Sometimes, he continued, 'jogging' the memory by exposure to significant people or articles from the past, helped in recovery.

He said blackouts were not uncommon after brain injury and that I needed special care till I healed completely.

After the doctor left the room there was complete silence. It was time to reveal everything.

I told Jessica that I had a girlfriend back in Delhi whose name was Manika. I told her about the conversation we had and all that I saw and did at MGM Grand and the casino.

I told her that I did not love Manika. It was just a relationship that we had drifted into. A halfhearted relationship.

And then I told her about the money.

I poured it all out.

I told her how I had been an aimless drifter - depressed and demoralized, until I woke up one day and found a 100 million dollars in my bank account.

I told her how Manika had confirmed that it was money that I had earned, though I had no recollection of how I did it.

I told her that the money had given me a new life but it was she who had given that life meaning. It was she, Jessica, who had taught me the meaning of love, the meaning of happiness.

She hugged me tightly, tears running down her face.

I could feel her love. I could sense her anxiety. I could tell, she cared.

Encouraged, I continued.

Manika had told me about my best friend who had died recently. I was clueless about this person. Had he come into my life after the amnesia had set in? Maybe that's why I didn't remember him at all.

Once again I started on the jigsaw puzzle of half remembered dreams. I tried making some connections, piecing all the stories and dreams together to get a picture of what had happened.

Was Abhi the guy with the gun? If he was my best friend, then why was he pointing a gun at me?

I remembered his words to me clearly:

"This plan will surely work. We've done the simulation a thousand times! I told you it would do the trick.

We did it, man! You were awesome!

100 million dollars in fifteen fucking days.

Goooooooooosebumps!"

I could see myself in the picture – in tears, overwhelmed at what I had pulled off. But what had we pulled off? A heist of some kind??

Then, why would Manika say that I had earned the money?

To recheck if I had come to this place, I opened my U.S citizen passport, it was a blunder, why I did not see my visit just two weeks before. It was written clearly, I had come to U.S 15 days back. How did I miss this?

To find the answers to these questions, I would have to go back to India.

I wanted to know how we made the money. I wanted to know who the guy with me was and why he had committed suicide. Why was Manika apologizing to me? What was the misunderstanding?

Jessica was not thrilled about my India quest. She feared it would be more damaging for me.

"I need to do this Jessica. I don't feel whole without the answers. I need to do it for both our sakes." I was firm. I was reluctant to take Jessica with me without knowing what dangers lay at the other end.

"Go back home and wait for me. I will be in touch with you every day. And when this is all over. I'll come to you, I promise." She wept. She didn't want to leave me.

But I had no option. Intuition told me that I was walking into danger by returning to India, yet I could not contemplate a life of half-truths and not knowing.

I couldn't live like that.

"Whatever happens, you and I are real. What we feel for each other is real. I will come back to you Jessica, this love will keep me alive."

In convincing Jessica, I was trying to convince myself.

But even while I made those statements my heart was filling with dread. I was swamped with a premonition that it would all end soon, but not well.

The world is at peace because we don't know what's coming next. Who knows if the breath we are inhaling right now, is our last one. Jessica was offering me a world of love and happiness, but it was also a world shrouded in ignorance and deception. When your mind is not at peace you can never be at peace.

In the days before I left for India, we clung together. We kissed like it was our last kiss. We made love like it was our last time. We couldn't get enough of each other. On our last night together, we stayed awake the whole night wishing that dawn would never come. But the chill of parting was upon us. I took her in my arms with great tenderness and wanted to protect her forever. I had never loved her more.

Was this the last meeting with my love? I prayed my intuition was wrong.

The coming days were crucial for me. They were either going to lead me to the answers, or lead me to my end.

Not all stories have a happy ending.

Chapter 9

The 100 Million Gamble

As soon as I reached Delhi, I asked Manika to meet me. She named a restaurant in Connaught place in central Delhi, and a time - 5 p.m. She asked if I had the money with me. I evaded the question. She asked if I was still angry with her.

Now that I had no clue about. Why was I angry with her?

She was obviously in the dark about my memory loss. Even if I couldn't remember much I could sense that something was wrong at her end. Was she dangerous for me? I had to take this meeting either way. She was the only lead I had.

Manika arrived on the dot but I was there even earlier. My suspicions had led me into doing an advance recce.

She was wearing a red tailored suit and appeared tense. By looking at her face I could tell she was desperately anxious.

As soon as she was seated she began apologizing.

"It was totally my fault. You trusted me and I let you down. Please forgive me." I got the feeling that her word were rehearsed and that her heart wasn't in it.

Forgive her for what? I remained silent.

"Don't try to act now Uday; you know why I am saying this." She was beginning to sound annoyed.

On an impulse I told her that I had a lapse in memory and I didn't recall anything about the money or the guy who had committed suicide. I knew telling her was a big risk to take, but I didn't see any other way.

I told her about the amnesia that had been caused by a blow to my head and the resultant swelling that had caused the memory loss. My cards were on the table.

"Manika, tell me again, how did I get a 100 million dollars? Who is Abhi?" I was impatient for the answers.

Her first response: "Do you still have the money with you? Did you remember where you kept it?"

She was looking at me disbelievingly. I could tell she did not trust me. But I still needed to get answers from her. So I showed my brain scans and the doctor's report.

As she started recounting the events that led to the hundred million, I could feel my memory return. I could remember who the man in my dreams was and how I'd met him. How we'd planned it all together.

I could remember everything but the last day. That memory was still elusive.

But, here it was - The 100 million dollar gamble!

Flashback

It was my birthday but as usual I had no plans to celebrate it. Like all other days this one too started with a cigarette and ended with a weed trip. The writing was on the wall. I was swiftly running out of money with no other revenue in sight. The situation was heading towards a desperate conclusion.

I had always loved playing cards for money.

Mom and dad forbade it, yet I persisted. One day I took Rs. 100 from my father's wallet, played cards with friends who were a lot older to me, and lost it all. I cried my heart out that day.

I was determined to win it back. I started pilfering small coins that my parents wouldn't miss and used it to gamble. That was the start of my addiction.

Mom and dad are not around anymore. It was my birthday and I was 100% sure that birthday luck was something I could rely on. But you can never tell in a game of cards.

Sometimes you win, most often you lose. That's how casinos are so profitable. The bar that I frequented had several chronic gamblers.

Some blew their entire wages and had to borrow money to feed their children, while some left laughing.

I was amongst those who usually lost money and came home drunk. But today was my day. I won a lot of money and for the first time, considered celebrating my birthday.

Just then a guy called Abhi joined the game. He sat calmly on his chair, poker faced, always looking at his cards with a half-smile. He observed each and every player at the table, carefully. He would often shift from one table to another. Every day, he kept a bit of his winnings for himself, the rest he donated to the poor children on the road. Many times he would quit the game when he was winning.

That day. The minute he joined my table, my luck began deserting me. I started losing money. All my birthday money went to him. Celebration cancelled! My mood crashed.

I was hopeless and on my way to being homeless. I had no reason to live.

Sitting alone with my dark thoughts I lit a cigarette. Cigarettes are a slow but classy way to commit suicide.

Suddenly I heard footsteps behind me and a voice said: "Poker is not gambling my friend. If you are playing poker and you look around the table and can't tell who the sucker is, it's you.

You rely on luck and nothing else. That's no way to play."

It was Abhi. He removed the cigarette from my hand, "It kills, man.

Can't you read it on the packet?"

"Who are you to advise me?" I asked. "I've had more experience than you can ever imagine, bro."

"It's not the experience," he said, "it's learning from the experience that matters. You are not a learner.

You should have learned the 'first rule of poker': Never get drunk while playing – but, look at yourself, you ass!"

"You have no fucking idea what I am going through in life." I blustered.

"Everyone has his or her own problems in life, my friend. It's how you deal with it," he said politely.

"Don't talk like you're God!" I was getting pissed off.

"No I can't be a God. God never speaks, he just show you the right path. If you change the way you look at things, the things you look at will change – believe me Bro!"

"As if you know everything about poker, man."

"Not everything, but many things. Enough to bleed idiots like you."

"Teach me your tricks then," I challenged.

"Okay, but on one condition. You will try to learn but not earn. Don't think about the money. It will automatically come."

"Deal!" I said.

His words resonated in my mind. My life changed after meeting him. He was always polite and happy. I could feel the positive aura around him. He radiated contentment.

"So let's start with the basics! The 7 tips to play poker.

The next time I see you within twenty meters of alcohol, I will beat the hell out of you." He threw all the beer out of my fridge.

"I can't live without it," I told him.

"Of course you can. You can live without anything you want. It's all in your head."

"Rule 1:

- Don't Play Drunk

  Your first big mistake. You may as well display your cards to everyone. Your reactions are visible to all. You are easily read. Never play like that

Rule 2:

- Do Fold More; Don't Play Every Hand.

Rule 3:

- Don't Bluff Just For Bluffing's Sake

  You know you suck at bluffing, yet you do it. At least try to camouflage your reaction.

  Everyone can sense it when you try to bluff.

Rule 4:

- Don't Stay in a Hand Just Because You're Already In It

  You will learn this with practice but remember this statement.

Rule 5:

- Do Pay Attention to the Cards on the Table

Rule 6:

- Do Pay Attention to the Other Players

Don't ever be self-centered in this game or you will lose it all in a single bet.

Rule 7:

✦ Don't Play at too High a Limit."

I began remembering all the tricks he had taught me. I remembered him saying:

"Never test the depth of the river with both feet. You will fall."

He used to relate his experiences to me, and all the situations that one could find in a poker game.

How different strategies are required for different situations.

It's a simple probability game.

A combination of luck and skill. People think mastering the skill is the hard part, but they are wrong. The trick to poker is mastering the luck.

I used to test my skills regularly.

Abhi taught me how to choose the table and which side to sit on, that offered the best vantage point to observe my opponents.

"Do the opposite of what everyone is doing and you will win. Or, wait for everyone to follow each other. Everyone will start playing like the one who wins some money in the beginning. Observe the patterns."

In a week I had mastered the game. We both used to play and formulate strategies to win.

We read a lot, and then more.

We practiced indicating our cards to each other through subtle eye movements. We got to know each other completely.

He would be the calm one in a game, and I would be the aggressor.

He told me that a poker tournament was held every year, with over million participants and the top ten winners were always the same. This proved that the game was not about luck.

Poker was NOT about luck!

I found a new aim in life, something new to learn.

This was the first time I started believing that I could be successful at something.

I used to practice continuously and search online for new tips. I scoured the poker blogs of the world champions. I watched videos of winners in action. I wanted to experience that feeling.

But the day when I first felt peace, and I'm talking real peace of mind, was when 'Abhi' came and took me to a place, which he called, 'the Heavenly Bench'.

He told me the story behind the term:

When Abhi was young he used to play football with his friends on a little flat hillock.

The whole place was windy and cold. There were big trees and bushes all around, the edges were very steep and one could see a beautiful sunrise from the bench.

On foggy mornings, the place looked ethereal. Sitting on the bench, with the fog playing around me feet and the cool breeze on my face, I felt like I was in Heaven. It was in this beautiful place that Abhi introduced me to meditation.

Whenever I opened my eyes after meditation I could see clouds and thick fog all around. That is why he called it the Heavenly Bench.

We began going there early, every morning, to experience its mesmerizing calm.

This was my best memory of the time spent with Abhi.

One night, I was reading an online book on poker when Abhi came in crying. He was totally devastated. I gave him a chair to sit on.

He told me about his mother. She had vomited blood and could not breathe properly. She was in a critical condition. She had been diagnosed with cancer six months ago. After that, he started playing poker in earnest, to pay for her treatment. She was in desperate need of a life-saving operation. But he needed money for that. More money than what he or I had.

The despair in his eyes and the lost look on his face reduced me to tears. I relived the day when I had seen my parents lying motionless, breathless and lifeless before me - a child who didn't even know the meaning of 'life', 'breath', 'death' and 'family.' A child who was yet to learn to speak in sentences had been sentenced to a life of loneliness.

I'd been too young to understand the reality of death. I had not even cried when my parents died and later, when

I was old enough, I got so used to that loveless, lonely life of mine,, that I never gave it another thought.

I made up my mind to help Abhi, not only for himself, but for that sweet little innocent who could do nothing to save his family.

Then a brainwave struck me. In a word - Manika. She was working in an MNC at quite a good post, and she was earning a decent salary. She was our only ray of hope. I dialed the magic numbers 9810******9 and there she was, at the other end of the line, stretching a helping hand forward, to lend us a sum of twenty lakhs.

That wasn't enough for the operation. We had to get more. Poker was my only talent and by now, Abhi and I had perfected out act well enough to win at any table.

We had a week to his mother's operation and I convinced him that we could make that money in Vegas in that time.

It was the biggest risk either of us had ever taken.

We believed we could win but the truth is, when the stakes are so high, and the life of your loved one depends on your game, then the pressure is bound to affect your focus.

Manika also wanted to come with us, as she too was involved and concerned. She knew Abhi from school and they even had some joint tuitions together. She wanted to be our cheerleader and support system.

The person I never really cared for, the person whose calls I answered only when I was in the mood, was coming through for me.

Manika arranged Abhi's and her visa using her contacts. She had an uncle working in the U.S. embassy.

Luckily I was born in the U.S and I could travel to most of the countries without a visa.

It was a very big step. But we had to take it. It was an issue of life and death for 'our' mother. The night before we left for Vegas, we met at the Heavenly Bench, Abhi, Manika and I.

I knew Abhi would want to come to this place before leaving. It was his temple. He used to meditate here for hours every morning which gave him the strength to face the day. It was the secret behind his positivity.

But meditation is not an easy thing to do. It's not easy to keep your mind from wandering when there are big issues at stake. Abhi was pre-occupied with his mother's condition.

The three of us sat on the bench talking till 5 a.m., almost time to leave for the airport.

Abhi wanted to pray there. There was no building, no idols of Gods, no priests, no bells, no incense.

Just a bench. A bench that had given him the best moments of his life. It was his temple, a temple for his mind, body and soul.

We sat there quietly just thinking about life. I could feel him mentally transmit energy to his mother, willing her to live for him.

Mind energy can be a powerful force. He was concentrating. His back straight, I could feel him taking deep breaths and saying, 'OM'.

Manika's eyes were also closed. She must have been thinking of how to take care of us both.

As for me, my mind was on the money. How much I would win and the kind of life I could buy with the money.

Try as I might, I could not divert my mind to anything else.

Chapter 10

VEGAS – The 100 Million Strategy

We converted all our cash to dollars. We had daily targets and once we reached it, we were determined to quit the table.

We resolved to stick to our strategies.

Abhi and I used to sit at the extreme ends of the table, to judge the players around.

I wore a suit every day and he dressed in casual clothes with a cap on.

Even the way you are dressed matters.

It shows your aggression and intent to play.

We used to shift tables at regular intervals and mark the weakest players at each.

We were clearing big sums every day.

I used to tip the guard outside the casino a 100 dollars, for his 'lucky smile' that cheered me.

We were winning big time. At the end of every day, Abhi called the hospital in India to check on how his mother was doing. She could not talk but he always asked the nurse to hold the phone to his mother's ears so that he could tell her how much he loved her. He used to cry a lot, but not on the phone. He always ended the call, saying, "I'm bringing the money ma, please wait for me."

He wanted to leave at once, when we had made enough money for the operation. But I forced him to stay on for few more days. We were on a roll, I told him. We could earn enough, not only for his mother's operation but to live in comfort for the rest of our lives. It was only a question of a few more days. We were a perfect team. There were no flaws in our strategy. After all those days and hours of practice it was payday!

Abhi reluctantly agreed to stay on for two more days. We split the winnings. I gave him the money for the operation, so that whatever happened, win or lose, that money would not be compromised. I kept the rest with me. I sympathized with Abhi, but my hunger for money always won out.

I used to count all of it at the end of the day. It made me ecstatic. The green note had a different feel to it. I couldn't get enough.

I wanted to play more. I wanted to win more. Abhi was afraid that if he stayed any longer, it might be too late for his mother. He just wanted to leave.

On our last day in Vegas, we got a call from the Casino owner. He invited us to play at the biggest table where businessmen from across the world, were playing. I forced Abhi to come and play.

The casino was rocking. There were ladies in miniskirts, sitting on the laps of businessmen.

We passed a board saying:

TEXAS HOLD' EM POKER

We were called into a different room. There were twenty people sitting at the table, who were amongst the richest poker-playing people in their respective countries.

We both sat at our pre-planned positions. Our plan was to win ten million dollars and leave the table.

Initially our strategies worked.

We were winning money until the dealer dealt a hand of cards that changed our lives.

He opened a Jack, Queen and a King of Hearts.

I had an Ace of Club but a Ten was missing. It could have been a straight flush otherwise.

My other card was forming a pair with a King.

The pot was getting bigger and bigger. No one was quitting the table.

The house dealer invited me to go all in with the money I had to take all the competitors out of the game.

The pot already had fifty million dollars!

I was observing the game very closely and everyone was following what other person was doing.

I decided to fold. So I took my five million and quit the game.

Abhi played on. The pot went to ninety five million and he was still in.

Abhi needed another five million to stay in the game. He asked the dealer if he could borrow it. The dealer agreed and I slipped him the money.

The pot reached its maximum limit

One hundred million dollars. The dealer said "Show!"

We won it royally with a ROYAL FLUSH.

We were the owners of a hundred million dollars!

"We did it man!"

"You were awesome!"

Abhi hurried to the hotel to pack his bags. I stepped outside.

I was on the top of the world. We had won a 100 million dollars.

We had earned it.

***

I could recall everything Manika was telling me. It was all true!

But there was some things that still eluded me.

I asked her why she kept apologizing to me.

She told me that it was because she had got engaged last week. Her family had pressured her into it.

She felt guilty as he hadn't been able to tell me in time.

Her phone rang. It was her fiancé calling and she said had to leave. She asked me once more about the money. There were still gaps in my knowledge. I didn't want to reveal anything about the money until I had all the answers. So I told her I didn't remember where I'd kept it. She clammed up after that. I kept peppering her with questions. What happened after we won? Where did we go? She either didn't know or didn't want to tell me.

Instead, she wanted me to concentrate on remembering where I'd kept the money; I evaded the question as I could sense something false in her manner. After that, she left in a hurry as her fiancé was waiting.

I puzzled over the unanswered questions.

I tried linking all the dreams together to figure out what was missing.

Flashback

"You want to kill me? Then shoot me, but I am not lying!"

I could see two people after the gunshot.

Chapter 11

The Incomplete Story

I knew something didn't ring true with Manika. The reason for her apology seemed lame.

I still could not recall what happened after we won the money.

I could remember my friend Abhi, and how we planned the whole venture. I remembered all that he taught me and how our strategies worked.

But Abhi committing suicide? That was not possible. That didn't gel with the Abhi I knew.

I tried calling Manika later but she was not picking up the phone. All I got from her was a text: 'Busy. Talk later.

Tell me about the money if you recall it.'

I texted back: 'I want to meet you.'

In reply, I got: 'Not possible. My fiancé is back.'

Definitely something was up there that didn't feel right.

I sat on a bench in a park lost in thought. I recognized the gunman as Abhi. Why was Abhi pointing a gun at me? Who else was there?

I had no clue at all. I began feeling vaguely depressed.

Firstly, I had squandered vast sums of money and now my best friend was no more. Why had he committed suicide?

I called Jessica.

She was relieved to hear from me. I told her everything that Manika had told me. She tried to cheer me up, said she knew everything would be good again. She was positive as always. How could she be so optimistic all the time?

My mind, on the other hand, was brimming with ominous vibes.

Jessica wanted to come to India to help me out with my situation, but I asked her to stay put. This was my problem and I would solve it.

I had to find the answers myself.

I went to the police station to make enquiries. I asked the policeman concerned I he could give me any information on the death of a person named Abhi who had died a few weeks ago.

The policeman said:

"Sir, the guy had gone completely mad.

He had returned from the hospital after seeing his mother's body and was found dead in the house. The house was completely burnt and so was he. We struggled to identify him.

Her mother was a cancer patient. She needed an operation which cost a lot. The son returned with the money but it was too late.

He could not handle the situation, sir. He would not take his mother home. He kept telling the doctors, 'I have the money with me. You do the operation, she will be well again.' She was dead but his hopes were not.

Sir, he was too disturbed. He did not want to perform the funeral rites for his mother. The hospital people managed to arrange for the last rites. He refused to even attend. They had to cremate her on their own. He did not come even after that.

He was too depressed over his mother's condition. Maybe that's why he missed spending the last few days with his mother. He was missing the entire last week of her life. The doctors repeatedly emailed him asking him to return before she breathed her last. His mother needed him. But he never came.

When he was found burnt at his home, his friend Manika took charge and organized the rituals. She didn't allow anyone to touch his body. She kept wailing that the purest soul had died. Everyone knew it was a case of suicide.

Manika ma'am immediately took him to the graveyard and performed all the rituals. She was profoundly upset."

I was in shock after listening to all of this.

The Abhi I knew was as a tough guy. Not suicidal at all. Had I been wrong about him?

I felt dejected and despondent. My best friend – why hadn't I helped him?

He had given me a reason to live, when I had nothing to live for. He gave me a goal when my life was aimless and in return, I seemed to have deserted him when he needed me most.

Distressed, I made my way to the graveyard to pay my respects.

I just asked someone where last rites are ritually performed, then sat at that place.

I could hear Abhi's voice saying:

"We are brothers from different mothers."

He would berate me whenever my attention strayed from the game. His pat on my back would cheer me whenever I felt low.

His teachings, his lessons, his positivity...

I would remember his words always:

Work for a cause, not for applause.

Live life to express, not to impress.

Don't strive to make your presence noticed, just make your absence felt.

I could feel his absence.

My best friend was gone from this world.

I called Jessica and wept on the phone.

I rarely cry but this time I sobbed whole-heartedly.

I let all the pain out.

I hadn't cried this much even when my parents died.

Why? Why hadn't I saved him?

Jessica wept with me. But she regained control and began calming me down.

I told her that I would come back to her soon.

That made her happy.

Gambling wins can never generate happiness. Happiness is generated by love.

I was now ready to leave everything behind for Jessica. All the unanswered questions, the puzzles of my past…

Once again she was my top priority.

Before I left I wanted to see the place where Abhi and I had done all our practicing, one last time.

I wanted to feel his presence there.

It was a small house in a small yard but it held millions of memories, cherished, dreams, desires, faith, loyalty, lessons, and friendship. Dwarka Sector 11 was where I had been taught the lessons of life, a place where I had found a shoulder to cry on, where I had been blessed with a master-philosopher-guide-parent and best friend – Abhi.

The land before my eyes was barren. It hadn't always been this way. There had been lush green bushes around, which were a refreshing sight after our intense practice sessions. That intoxicating fragrance of wet soil that entrances everyone, from infant to senior, had not left us untouched either.

We used to park ourselves on a blissfully romantic park bench, planning how we would be Masters of the Game, one day.

Abhi never allowed me to think about money, but my plans were always different.

His words still echoed in my mind. "Money is just a fake pleasure, real happiness is in your brain."

I wasn't just hearing this in my mind. Somebody had whispered it.

My body tingled all over with goosebumps. I felt a form to my right, standing with arms crossed in dominance.

Just like he used to.

He was right there, unseen but just felt, Abhi.

His presence was something I was yearning for with every iota of my body.

There was a security guard by the house. I asked for the keys. The guard studied at me, rheumy grey eyes peering out from a cobweb of wrinkles. Those infinitely tired eyes reflected the desolate hopelessness of the place.

A tiny teardrop, responding to gravity, splashed down on the parched soil.

The door opened.

It was all black and completely burnt – walls, broken ceilings. The place was completely destroyed but the table was still there.

I ran towards that round wooden table, as I used to, in a hurry to bag the best seat first.

"I choose this one," I shouted in excitement," ha! Now you choose yours. It's my game today."

Then it hit me with full force. Where was my friend? Why couldn't I see him anymore? Why wasn't he choosing his seat? Why wasn't he warning me about being over confident? Why wasn't he cursing me? Where was my friend???? Where?

I could see that, I was not a real player.

The real player had died.

"Why are you crying, beta?" The guard put a comforting hand on my trembling shoulder.

"He was dearer to me than father, mother or God."

I could not reply to the guard.

"Are you his brother?" he quavered.

I replied, swallowing my tears:

"No. I am his friend."

In a voice soft with wisdom, he said:

"Friends like you can only be found with luck, my son."

The guard's voice reverberated inside me.

Someone else had said this to me at the same place.

It was Abhi.

He had said it right here, standing before this very table. I had been standing on the other side.

The memories came crowding back.

Scene after scene. I remembered it all.

It felt like someone was repeatedly stabbing a knife into my head.

I fell to my knees. My head was exploding.

It was not a suicide, it was murder.

THE FINAL FLASHBACK

I stayed on my knees, listening to the voices in my head. It was my last conversation with Abhi.

My hands were cold; my body was getting numb. My head was pounding with the epiphany:

It was not a suicide; it was murder.

The guard helped me stand and took me outside. He gave me some water to drink but I could barely swallow.

My limbs were not cooperating. I was catatonic.

I could not feel my body.

Sometimes when you've had a great shock your body freezes and time stops.

Now time had stopped for me. Everything had stopped for me.

I had betrayed to the most loyal person on earth.

I was wracked with emotion.

I had no place to go. No place deserved me.

It was late at night. I wanted to call Jessica.

I want to tell her, she didn't deserve a low-life like me. No one did.

She picked up the phone.

Her voice was as enchanting as always.

I had given her enough pain.

I found I couldn't give her more. She asked me why I was sounding low.

I told her about Abhi, how good our friendship was and how dear he had been to me.

"Uday the longer you stay there, the more depressed you will become.

What had to happen, happened. Some things are beyond our control.

We are just an insignificant specks in an infinite Universe. You have to bear it and move on."

Words were frozen in my throat. I could not bring myself to destroy her positive impression of me with my story. I wanted to keep listening to her voice. It was bringing me peace.

How charming she sounded in her ignorance. How innocent. Silent tears continued to stream down my face, but I said nothing to her.

Tears were rolling down my cheeks.

I was crying! But it won't help me now.

Nothing can help me now.

I didn't want her to worry about me anymore.

I didn't want her to hear me crying.

I went to the 'Heavenly Bench' from where Abhi and I had watched many a sunrise.

Friends like him can only be found with luck and friends like me can only be found with bad luck.

It was 3 a.m. I was shivering with cold.

I wished someone could erase my memory. Hadn't I changed as a person, since?? Hadn't my life changed after that day?

Now that I could recall everything, I realized what money could do to a person.

Chapter 12

Payback

I was never a good learner. In spite of all Abhi's lectures, I stubbornly continued to believe that it was not all strategy in poker, sometimes you had to rely on luck.

Abhi was always a keen observer, quick to fold when his cards were not good. I used to play on and win sometimes, and poke fun at him for leaving the game too quickly. But he never retaliated.

He was a polite and a graceful player.

The day he came to me crying over his mother, I could not bear to see him in tears. I had no option but to call Manika. Till then, I had never had strong feelings for Manika. But that day, I felt my feelings change.

I had not expected her to be so forthcoming in my time of need. She just left her office instantly and rushed to our aid. She had emptied her savings and borrowed more to help me.

It made me feel ashamed. Compared to her generosity, how stingy I had been with my time and attention.

Sometimes a little help from a person changes your perspective and this was not just a 'little' help. She was even prepared to accompany us for support. She couldn't have done more.

I was deeply touched.

I fell in love with her. I believed she loved me too.

We went to Vegas and everything went exactly as planned.

We won a lot. We had daily targets set by Abhi. Once those were reached we tried to exit without getting too greedy.

Abhi was very smart. He was always one step ahead. Manika and I began to observe his game more deeply. Sometimes my bluffs didn't work and I would lose huge amounts, but calm, competent Abhi was always our savior at the end of the day.

Once we had made enough for the operation, Abhi wanted to leave. He was desperate to go back to his mother. I was the one who pressurized him into staying for a few more days.

Manika was better at handling him when he got emotional. Long after I had left the room she would be sitting with him holding his hand, reassuring him that everything would work out well.

I did get a little jealous but by then, I loved and trusted her completely. After all, hadn't she demonstrated her love for me by rushing to my aid?

Besides I was always thinking about how to make more money. I loved counting the dollars we made. I loved the money we won.

On the final day we had set a target of ten million and were determined to quit once the target was reached.

Our carefully laid plans were blown apart as the game snowballed into one of the biggest challenges in our lives.

Abhi knew that our fellow players had deep pockets and that we would be tempted to play on.

From the start the bets were very high. The pot kept growing. We knew how to signal each other discreetly. We could indicate our hand with subtle gestures, so that the other could decide whether to quit or play. Abhi wanted me to up the ante so that everyone else would back out and we could clear ten million. But I knew he held a dream hand, the best cards one could have in the game, so I disregarded his strategy and folded. Everyone else put their money in and the pot became ninety five million. I lent him the other five and the rest was history.

It was our luck that worked that day.

It was my strategy. We aimed for ten million but won a hundred million.

It was my 100 million.

I deserved it more than him.

I drank whole night. I was happy and I was high.

Disaster struck.

Abhi had to return immediately to India. Doctors had declared his mother dead.

Abhi was in shock. He needed help, sympathy and support, but I was not ready to sympathize. I wanted to enjoy my victory. I was very high.

It was all about the money for me. I had never seen such an amount in my life and I would see it again.

I couldn't help being thrilled.

I could buy a new life with this kind of money. A life where everything would go my way.

I could buy anything, any person. It was my world now.

When I eventually headed back to our room, I could hear whispering from within.

I opened the door.

I anticipated gasps of excitement or sorrow. Instead there were different kind of gasps and a different kind of excitement in the room. My girl and my best buddy were in each other's arms gasping for more.

Manika was all but hidden behind Abhi. She was against the wall with her arms around Abhi's neck, straining towards his head, desperate to deepen the contact. Her feet danced restlessly in her hunger for closeness. Her eyes, filled with wild wanting dreams.

The sight pierced me to my heart.

I turned away from the door. Manika followed, calling my name. I fled the hotel.

I was livid with anger. My face burned red, my eyes burned hot. I felt betrayed. Abhi had let me down in the worst possible way. He had taken my girlfriend from me.

I had all the money, I reminded myself. I am the winner and he is the loser.

When I returned to the hotel I found that they had already left for India. Both of them.

They hadn't cared enough to make a single call to me. Manika was equally responsible for all this.

I could not bear the thought of them together.

Did they think they were going to get away with it? Live happily ever after leaving me in the dust? No way!

I had been insulted. I had been cheated. I had been taken advantage of. Now it was my turn. It was my time. I was going to return the favor.

The time was right and I had the perfect excuse to teach my master a lesson. I had the perfect weapon as well.

Being master of those gorgeous greenbacks, the only master, I had the power to decide his future.

I went back to India the next day, and deposited the money in my international bank. I met the bank manager and put in enough security so that no one else could ever access my bank account.

I had earned the money and with me it would stay. Those who betrayed me would get no part of it.

But what would Abhi do if I withheld his share? He could reveal my secret to the media. He could get me into trouble with the revenue authorities. There was only one option. He had to be taken out of the picture.

He stole my girlfriend and in return, I would steal his life.

Money changed me completely. It turned me into a raging megalomaniac with no control.

It's the worst thing in the world is to see your lover and your best friend, making love. I replayed the image, feeding my rage.

Each time it felt like being stabbed in the heart.

My reaction was extreme and now my payback would also be extreme.

I called a guy who used to play poker with me at the bar. I heard he was a hit man with 8-9 murders under his belt.

I had avoided the bastard before, but now I was looking for him.

I hired him to kill Abhi.

Abhi called me up that day, and asked to meet me at his home, where we used to practice. He wanted me to bring the money we had won.

It messed me up. Why should I give him the money?

He was a real loser and a cheater. He backstabbed me.

But, it was a good chance to kill him.

I gave the murderer the time and place and handed over his payment

I had gone mad with the money, I had. I was high on weed and I could do it all my life. I had enough money to buy any drug, experience anything and fuck any girl.

I waited for the guy to give me the news of the murder and I got a call.

It was from Manika.

She was crying loudly, "Sorry Uday. I'm really sorry. What can I say? I've always been attracted to Abhi. He is always polite and steady, not selfish like you. He is everything a girl needs.

You were always thinking about money and not me.

Money matters to you more than love.

Did you think it was you I came running to help? We hardly had that kind of relationship. It was for Abhi. But he only saw me as your friend. Until the day his mother died.

I was the one who kissed Abhi and seduced him that day. He was all I wanted. He cared for his mother and he cares for every person around him.

When his mother died, you have no idea how much he suffered.

He was alone! He needed you. But you were lost to him – only interested in celebrating the money.

He needs your support now. Go to him."

I was stricken. I had got it all wrong. It was my misunderstanding. There was no time to waste. I hoped I was not too late.

We had shared everything together but I had been ready to doubt him.

Money had made me blind. I knew now that he would never have betrayed me.

What the hell had I done?

I reached his home. The gate was open. I prayed that I had made it in time. My heart was thundering. I had to get him out of there. I began looking for him everywhere.

Then I heard a voice filled with bitterness:

"You were never a true friend. I knew it. It was all about money for you. Why did I have to help you? Why did I trust our friendship, if this is what you want to do?"

Abhi was crying. But his hands were steady. He held a gun in them and it was aimed at me.

"I am sorry Abhi. I misunderstood you completely. This is not what I want."

"You want to kill me? Then shoot, but I am not lying!"

I said looking into Abhi's eyes.

"You sent a man to kill your best friend because of the money. You have learnt nothing Uday. You were never a learner.

You were always a greedy bastard. You took the life of my mother Uday, you forced me to stay on and I could not save her. Yes! It was you, who murdered my mother… and now, you've sent a man to kill me.

Shame on you Uday!

Friends like you can only be found with luck, bad luck!"

Gunshot.

The bullet hit something behind me. At the same time something hit me at the back of my head. As I went down I saw that the hired assassin had entered the room.

"Don't kill Abhi," were my last words before I blacked out.

I had killed my friend.

I was the murderer.

It was my doing.

I wondered how I had got back home after I had blacked out. I figured that the killer must have burnt the house with Abhi in it, to make it look like a case of suicide. The police would never catch him. They weren't even looking for him.

Had he been the one to take me home and leave me in my room to start this 100 million journey?

I had woken up with a frightful headache and no memory of the past two weeks, and then I had found the money in my account.

Now my memory of the events was complete.

Remembering didn't make me feel better, though.

I was a killer.

I lost my best friend.

I was a cad who had never cared about love.

I was all about the 100 million dollars.

Chapter 13

Peace at the Heavenly Bench

Sitting on the 'Heavenly Bench' I began sending Jessica a long text.

The whole story of what happened before I met her. I held back nothing.

How I'd become such a bastard after getting the money.

All my flaws, my cheats, my lies, my regrets, my greed, the darkness in me…I confessed it all.

This was the place where I had the best memories of Abhi. This was where Abhi, Manika and I had spent the night together, before leaving for Vegas. Our last few hours of innocence, hope and togetherness.

Abhi had brought me here to introduce calm and meditation into my life.

I was always a hyperactive guy looking for a quick buck – a short-cut to success. This was the only place where I found peace. I breathed in the pure air and felt the soothing power of nature and the essence of Abhi's positivity surround me.

Trees all around, a view of hills and a cold marble bench for three.

I wanted to cleanse all my sins at this place. I wanted forgiveness.

The message was composed. I hit 'send'.

It was 3:27 am.

My eyes were wet. I still could not believe that it was I who was the culprit, the murderer. I had not been able to enjoy life, even with all the money in the world. I had been tortured endlessly by those dreadful dreams and restlessness. Even when my mind had erased the dreadful memories, my subconscious had kept them alive. You can never fool your brain. It is the seat of intelligence.

I didn't want to fool anybody anymore. The person who changed me for the better, needed to know what I was, even if she didn't accept me after hearing the truth.

Jessica deserved to know that person who was responsible for her happiness had never been good for anyone or anything, before she met him.

I had wasted my whole life pondering ways to fill my wallet. Money was the only reason I kept gambling. And I gambled shamelessly. I spent my nights losing bets at roadside liquor shops, even going on to placing a few treasured possessions of my parents on the line, just to make a quick buck.

And for what?

That extra can of beer to wet my throat, as it went dry while watching a shameful amount of porn? Or that call girl in a miniskirt I came across in the 'galli' where a guy peddled hashish? I don't remember the things I made her do while I was stoned to the core, lying in a dump that I called my room. Hell, I don't even remember her face.

My hunger for money was insatiable. I believed money could buy me a life. A better life. And I was ready to forgo anything for it. Anything. I hadn't wiped the dust off my parents' photograph for days. I hadn't closed my eyes and remembered them as they were. Pure, true people. Oh, Papa, I remember you. I should have listened to you. Ma, I shouldn't have let you take my side. Let him slap me, Ma. Let him slap that little pick-pocketing truant so that he can grow up to be a better human. That's what the both of you always wanted, didn't you?

Each and every moment of that life when I was emotionless, heartless and aimless, flashed before my eyes.

How rude I had been to Manika.

I remembered the first evening when I had taken her hand and led her to the terrace of the college building. I had stood on the ledge and screamed into the night air, Bollywood style: "Tu kahe to iss chath se main haste haste koond jaoon. Tujhe mein itna pyaar karta hoon, meri jaan."

I remembered how she'd pulled me off the ledge and slapped me till my cheeks stung. And then she'd held me in her arms and sobbed endlessly. Ah, the silence that followed. Ah, that touch of hers. Her jet-black hair dancing in the night wind. Her pale face turning red as she sobbed her heart out. She loved me to death. As for me, I reduced her importance in my life to that of the ATM machine across the street. A mere convenience.

She wasn't wrong to caress Abhi that night. Both were in need of some support, some care, some love. And I took that away from them.

I never gave her anything, why did I expect her to give me her all?

Whatever you do, it all comes back to you.

This is what we call the truth of Karma.

I had never understood her feelings. Never cared for her.

She was right. No one would like to be with selfish me. At that moment I forgave her for hurting me.

In procuring a better life for myself, I never knew that the price I would pay would be the lives of the only people who had given me a reason to live.

Sitting on that bench I was in pain.

Jessica should know that her lover had murdered the nicest guy in the world. A guy who would do anything for his mother. A guy who had cheered everyone around him with his presence.

I killed him. I killed his mother.

I killed what was best in humanity.

I had never learnt the meaning of happiness. Abhi was right.

I was never a good learner.

I could recall each and every person, whom I had let down without a second thought. There were many.

I could see all their faces in the sky.

My mom, dad, Jessica and Abhi.

I did not have the courage to face them.

Sitting on the bench, I traveled to an imaginary world where only feelings were real. The world of my parents and Abhi. I apologized to them, for being such a cheater, with joined hands and tears running down my face. I promised to be true, not just to people around me, but also to my own self. I promised to work hard and earn wisely.

I told them about Jessica and how happy I was with her, how relaxed and carefree, how contented she made me feel with every touch of hers.

It was reincarnation, a new life, a new phase, a new ME… as a loyal human being.

I wanted them to give me another chance at life.

I could feel all three of them in the sky, watching me.

I wished money could buy me eternal sleep, so that I could sleep away my sins, my weaknesses and my guilt. "Help me out, Abhi. Just this one last time, Bhai. I promise I'll pay attention."

I lost my composure and wailed like a baby, hiding my face in my hands. I felt alone, empty.

"Wipe the tears off my face, Ma. Can you, please?"

No, I need to be strong. I have wronged the ones who loved me and probably, truth is the only way to make it up to them.

Now I have my love with me.

My true love Jessica.

I have confessed to her, all the blunders of my life.

I will live up to my promises now.

The only way to live a happy life is to be true to yourself.

I will go to the police.

I will be a good man like Abhi.

Yes I can.

God has given me one more chance.

Jessica will forgive me.

I can remember every moment we spent together.

I will cherish each one.

I had got one more chance to live!

It was time lead a happy, truthful life with my partner.

They were all in the sky but totally silent. My father, mother and Abhi.

I willed them to respond. I yearned for a sign.

They were all very quiet.

It was 4:15 and it was still dark. The mist hung all around me.

I felt a lot lighter. Maybe the truth wasn't so painful after all. A smile spread across my face as I contemplated the night sky. I took several calming breaths as I gazed at the little speckles of white in the dark expanse of the sky above.

I wished I was holding Jessica's hand. We would sit silently till the piercing rays of the dazzling sun tore down the dark curtains, like I wished the rays of truth would pierce the curtain of my dark deeds and usher in a new day for me.

A new beginning for us.

Oh, how I wish Jessica you were here to see the sunrise with me.

I wanted to call and hear her voice. But it was late. She would be fast asleep.

Then subtly, the darkness turned menacing.

The harsh hoots of the night owl sounded eerie.

Somewhere a dog began to howl mournfully.

Even the trees seemed to shudder, holding their leaves closer for protection.

It was like all nature was giving me a warning.

My phone beeped.

It indicated that my message had been read.

I felt light. Now Jessica knew everything.

My truth was received... my message was received.

Wait a minute…message received…received by… by…Manika!

I had mistakenly send the message to Manika instead of Jessica. It had been read by Manika half an hour ago.

I could see the message screen blinking.

Manika had replied:

"Don't worry Uday, I have forgiven you everything. I'm happy that you now remember it all. I have almost reached you. Just wait for me."

I had not wanted to let her know about the money and my role in Abhi's murder.

I was very nervous now.

I heard footsteps behind my bench.

Manika had arrived.

She was wearing a skirt and white top. She came and sat beside me. There was a strange expression in her eyes.

I was embarrassed to face her.

It was I who had killed our best friend. They had both been very close in the last few days of Abhi's life.

She must hate me. I apologized to her and put my heart into it.

I was mortified.

She asked me again: "Where is the money, Uday?"

I stayed silent.

She laughed, "You were always that selfish Uday."

Again I sensed something was wrong.

Her phone rang. It was her fiancée calling.

She cut the call without answering. I told her to take it.

"Why did you come here at this time? He must be worried."

"He's not worried, Uday. In fact, he's here."

Someone came up from behind, put his hands on my shoulder and swiftly sat on the bench by my side. A cap covered his face.

It was the same cap.

He pulled it off.

"Hey brother! This is cheating now. You should at least share the money with us."

That someone was Abhi.

CHAPTER 14

Money is Everything

I reeled in shock. I could not believe what was happening. My heart began to hammer. It was surreal. My mind has been playing a lot of games with me, perhaps this was another one?

"You are the real winner. Hats off!"

Abhi ceremoniously placed his cap on my head.

"Boss, you win, I lose.

THE 100 MILLION DOLLAR winner!"

He took a cigarette from a pack and lit up.

He offered me one too. I stopped him.

"I know what you're thinking. You're wondering that the man who took the packet from your hand is offering it to you again.

Take it this time brother. Life changes.

It's not going to harm you now. You are already hurt badly."

Ha-ha! He laughed and Manika followed.

They both were looking at the sky and laughing out loud.

"You are such a fool, Uday. So predictable.

'Tu chutiya hai ek number ka.'

God did not give you a brain and when you thought you had one, he took away all memory from you."

"How do you know I lost my memory? Did Manika tell you?"

"Ha! We both knew it even before you came to know.

This darling, sitting beside you hit you so hard on your head that you lost your memory." He turned to Manika and continued:

"Manika, I told you to hit him just hard enough to knock him out, but you clobbered him on the most important part of his brain. The part that was required for us to know where he kept the money."

Manika felt the back of my head. "Did it really hurt that bad?"

Her laughter followed.

"You know something Uday, every time I told you, I'm so sorry because you lost your memory, I was actually wishing I had hit you harder. You deserve harder than that.

You were so stupid you never understood why I was apologizing. I knew if I did it often enough you would come back here to find out why. So I went on apologizing. And what did you do? Come right back here too find out why I was saying sorry to you.

Actually, I am now really feeling sorry for you.

Look at you, my silly boy."

A shock wave went straight through my body from brain to toe. I sat rooted to the spot, trembling slightly.

I was beyond emotion.

Unbelievable! I had been cheated and backstabbed. I had been played.

One moment I had been full of regret about how I had treated Abhi, and now here he was, gloating about how he had cheated me!

"By the way, where did you call me from?" Manika asked.

"I was in Vegas," I replied.

"Did you go there again to play, you selfish piece of shit?" Abhi asked.

"You know what Uday; idiots like you rarely survive. You are an exception. You're an idiot with a 100 million dollars.

This was all planned, my hero! Manika and I planned it. At least you should have taken care of your girlfriend, man. She is hot but you never cared for her. Everyone loves money but you should respect women at least."

Manika came around and sat on Abhi's lap. "Yes you should have taken care of me Uday. I would have been sitting on your lap instead."

She took the cigarette from his hand and took a deep drag. She blew the smoke on my face laughing.

"You did not care about Manika that became my biggest asset. She knew you would care for her even less, after winning the money. Such a lovely girl you missed out on, she just needed love, Uday."

"Baby, no one can take you from me." He kissed Manika on her neck, put his hands on her thighs and they locked lips.

"You should not smoke, it kills. I can't see the hottest chick on earth dying." Abhi said to Manika.

They were both different. I had never seen them this way.

"So the money has changed you too," I said.

"I changed you into the good brother and you changed me into the bad one. A really bad one. But we are equal now. We are both changed." Abhi continued.

"Before you, I had never seen a man so emotionless, so hungry for money. I learnt that from you.

You taught me to be selfish. You taught me how to survive in this cruel world.

I knew you would kill me if you could. But I was way smarter than you are.

It all started when you were high after winning. As soon as we got the news about my mother's death I wanted us to go back at once, but did you care? Manika was my only support. She was on my side."

"C'mon Abhi, I was always on your side.

You were smarter, way smarter than this fool." Manika said.

"You went out to party that night and Manika was there with me in our hotel. We had to take the money from you. But we did not want to be villains. That is your role.

You saw us kissing and craving for love that day in our hotel. You know why we did it? To manipulate you.

You're such a predictable shit.

We knew you would come rushing back to Delhi in search of me. To take revenge. To fight for your love who is now mine.

I knew how to make you jealous enough to make a misstep. That is exactly what you did. Right?

I provoked you even more by demanding my share. I knew you were money-minded. You would do anything but share.

You were afraid that I would reveal your secrets to the police.

I tapped your phone. You called the killer from that phone. You walked into our trap you dumb ass.

Just when you were waiting for the killer to call and give you the good news of my murder, I asked Manika to call you.

Oh you loser! You cannot kill me. Your brain has been taught and trained up by me. You can't outsmart me.

You believed it all: That is was she who seduced me and that I was the innocent party.

Well, look into these innocent eyes.

Look into my eyes, you bastard.

You wanted to kill me. You? Look at you? You are already a dead body. How can you kill anyone?

Your brain did not let you sleep in peace even after having a 100 million dollars.

Oh look at, you poor spoiled brat!

We should have killed you right there at my home.

But that bloody killer appeared at the right moment and I shot at him. Manika hit you at the back of your head at the right time.

We thought you would wake up and tell us where you've kept the money. But you didn't.

We had to burn the house with the killer's body. We were afraid that the police would ask questions. Here again, my darling did the job for us. She convinced the police that the body was mine and quickly cremated it.

They were sympathetic because my mother had died.

My mother's death saved us. I loved my mother, I could not save her but she saved me."

Abhi stood up and slapped me hard on my face; I could feel the heat, the strength of his slap.

"You killed my mother, you.

Your selfishness killed my mother. You didn't let me come back early when we already had enough money for her operation.

You were greedy for more.

This is what makes you the most fucked up person on earth."

I was numb and he continued talking.

"It was you who was the source of all our problems. We just wanted to kill you and take the money. We deserved it, not you. We waited for you to wake up and tell us where it was.

But you, you idiot, was still knocked out after the blow.

Manika even took you to the hospital. Sorry brother, I could not come because I was 'dead' to the world.

The doctor told her that your memory had gone and that the only way it would return, was if you were left to lead a normal life.

So we had to take you, the owner of 100 million dollars, back to that shitty house.

But, you recovered physically, quicker than we expected and you flew away. You lucky-ass.

You have no idea how long we have been waiting for those green gorgeous greenbacks.

So have you learnt the final lesson of your life???

Speak up? Bol chutiye.

Never trust anyone when it comes to a 100 million dollars."

HAHAHAHAHAHAHAHAHAHAHA!

"But now it's time to part with it.

I was the mastermind. I was the planner.

I gave you life Uday, accept it.

You would have died if I had not helped you.

It was I, your father, your God, and your boss.

NOW give my share back to me.

Give us our share." He pulled out a gun and pointed it at me.

"By the way how much have you spent till now?

Don't tell me you lost it in Vegas, without me.

Hahaha!

You can never win that game without my advice."

I wiped my tears; I had lost all faith in humanity.

I had been searching for happiness among the wrong people. I had taken the most twisted man on this earth, to be my God.

I had been a poor judge of people. And this lack of judgement had brought me this - to death's door.

I had lost all hope. I had lost all illusions about faith, trust and friendship.

When blood-brothers can kill each other, why wouldn't Abhi kill me?

We were brothers from different mothers, like he used to say.

Mankind is flawed. We let money destroy all that's fine in human nature.

I walked to the edge of the cliff and stood there feeling the wind. The wind pummeled me.

The fury of nature hit me hard. Really hard.

Manika and Abhi watched me warily.

"Don't jump brother; your life is precious for us. It is worth a 100 million dollars," Abhi laughed.

"I don't have any money now," I said. "Not a cent."

He was shocked.

"Yes it's all gone.

Gone to a place where you cannot reach it ever."

They both stood silently watching me.

Manika came forward and put her hands on my chest,

"Won't you even tell me about it? C'mon Uday. You loved me once. Tell us where the money is. We'll divide it equally. We are not as selfish as you are."

I put my arms around her, trapping her hands.

She began to struggle. "Let go Uday; you don't have the right to touch me now."

Abhi stood there smirking.

"He can't do anything Manika. He is a loser.

A 100 million dollar loser, I should say."

"You won't ever get the money Abhi.

You took all the love away from my life.

Now it's time for me to take your love."

Holding Manika in my arms and thinking of Jessica, I stepped off the cliff.

I felt light, I felt totally relaxed.

I felt weightless; I could see moments with Jessica flash in front of my eyes.

Love never dies; it's in your soul.

And the soul is eternal.

Death is peaceful. Death is oblivion.

Epilogue

Jessica was waiting for Uday's call.

She was worried.

She was packing her bags to come to India but she had no idea where to go.

She had woken up with a start, with the sound of Uday's scream ringing in her ear.

She could feel he was gone.

Her love was gone.

God has His own way of telling people about loss.

She receives a parcel with a letter in it.

It is from Uday.

To my love Jessica,

By the time you get this, I have no idea whether I will be alive or not, but this I do know: I don't deserve this wealth which God has blessed me with.

I found my real wealth when I met you.

I know you will use this money to help those who really need it.

You will live in my soul forever.

Miss your smile.

UV